D1172078

#4

Nowlan, Alden

Various persons
named Kevin O'Brien.

#4

Nowlan, Alden

Various persons
named Kevin O'Brien.

various persons named kevin o'brien

a fictional memoir

alden nowlan

clarke, irwin
& company limited
toronto, vancouver
1973

© 1973 by Clarke, Irwin
& Company Limited

ISBN 0-7720-0588-5

1 2 3 4 5 6   JD   78 77 76 75 74 73

Printed in Canada

contents

acknowledgements

The Atlantic Advocate
The Brunswickan
Event
The Fiddlehead
The Journal of Canadian
    Fiction
Jewish Dialogue
Prism International
The Tamarack Review
University of Windsor Review
West Coast Review
One segment was previously
published in the anthology
Fourteen Stories High edited
by David Helwig and Tom
Marshall and published by
Oberon Press; another seg-
ment was previously pub-
lished in the anthology
Contemporary Voices edited
by Donald Stephens and
published by Prentice-Hall
of Canada Limited.

for claudine,
johnnie
and leo
with love

Perhaps I should begin this book with a page containing nothing except a question mark. As a child I ached to put the question into words, but never could. Nor can I find the proper words for it now. That child, Kevin O'Brien, would stop whatever else he was doing when he felt the question returning. He would press his chin against his knees, screw his eyes shut and tighten his fists on his temples like the two halves of a vice: doing to his body what I, the man Kevin O'Brien, do to my mind.

Probably it's a mistake to call it a question, since that implies that there could be an answer, and maybe it's a mistake to refer to it at all, since by its very nature it refuses to be put into words, and therefore anything I or anyone else may say about it will be more or less a lie.

But it's a little like this: a dumb aching wonder at how strange it is to be here inside this body and in this world. It's somewhat as if I had awakened in a stranger's body on another planet. Or, and this may be closer to the truth, it's as though I were dreaming and knew I was dreaming but couldn't remember who I was or where I lived when I was awake.

1

rumours
of war

There are no chance visitors to Lockhartville. You
arrive there by turning off one road and then another and
another, as if you were a child playing snakes and ladders.
And each road is a little lonelier and a little narrower and
a little rougher than the previous one. There are no signs
to direct you, only maps drawn to too small a scale, and
memories that have become increasingly detached from
geography.

Lockhartville is one of those villages (if a few houses
that happen to be situated along a four-mile stretch of dirt
road can be called a village) that are more isolated now
than they were fifty years ago. The passenger trains have
ceased to run through. The main highways have bypassed
not only the village itself but the nearest towns. The dairy
trucks no longer come from the city every weekday
morning to pick up cream cans and hitch-hikers. The sawmill has been permanently shut down. Men whose fathers
crossed the continent to harvest wheat or sailed schooners
to the West Indies now stay at home and wait for their
welfare and family allowance cheques from the government.
The presence of television only serves to widen the gap
between Lockhartville and the rest of the world, since little
or nothing that appears on the screen has the remotest
connection with what can be seen from the window.

For the returning native Kevin O'Brien Lockhartville
is not fixed in present time as other places are. What
happens to him there is almost independent of calendars, so
that there are frequent moments when it is as if he were a
ghost returning into the past to spy upon one or another
of his former selves.

As we first perceive this ghostly Kevin O'Brien he is

driving a rented car from the motel where he registered
a few hours ago toward the house in which he was born
and where his father still lives. This Kevin O'Brien now
makes his home in another part of the country, where he
works for a newspaper. Since his newspaper has assigned
him to cover a story in a city within easy driving distance
of his birthplace, he has decided to go for a visit and has
arranged to take a few days off in order to do so. Three,
five, perhaps even ten years have elapsed since his last visit
—he prefers to leave the length of the interval vague even
in his own mind, because this is one of those instances
when vagueness is more truthful than accuracy. In the
truest sense of all, Lockhartville is not a real place, but a
verbal convenience, a quick, easy and perhaps lazy way of
denoting a certain set of experiences that possess a unity
more easily sensed than defined.

I'd better keep my mind on the road, he thinks, as the
car swerves dangerously on an ice patch: he had applied
the brakes too vigorously on an unexpected curve.
There is a thin blanket of snow under the trees that
line either side of the road: tall, skeletal trees growing
so close together that their roots suck the life out of one
another, and each one is prevented by its neighbours from
gaining access to the sun. Good-for-nothing trees. Gro-
tesquely overgrown weeds. Trees, and poles strung with
telephone and electric power lines. He can remember
the time twenty years or more earlier when these same
poles or their predecessors were raised by men who later
climbed them with spurred and spiked boots and then
leaned far back high above the earth in their safety belts, as
enviable as sailors on the masts of a square-rigger in a
picture book. And as a boy he lay awake many nights
listening to the bittersweet music these wires made when
they were strummed by a cold wind off the north Atlantic.
When you're very young there's music in the air you
breathe.

The poles were raised because of the war, and the RCAF
Flying Training School that the war brought with it. For
a while, again because of the war, Kevin's father had

4

earned five or six dollars a day for working at the airport as a carpenter's and plumber's assistant, as compared with the thirty dollars a month he had been paid for cutting pulpwood during the Depression. I must drive out to the airport before I leave, Kevin says to himself. It was a central part of his childhood and youth. The flying school was closed, the airport abandoned and most of the buildings sold, torn down and taken away immediately after the war. On Kevin's last visit the grass had already prevailed over the cement runways to such an extent that from a little distance away it would have been difficult for a stranger to detect that anything man-made had ever existed there, although such a stranger might have wondered why the ground there was so flat and treeless while the countryside all around it consisted of woods and hills.

It begins to snow; he fumbles for the switch of the windshield wipers and turns them on. He recalls how, after the airport was abandoned but before the runways had given way to the grass, he and a beautiful girl named Annie Laurie MacTavish rode across it one afternoon on their bicycles and in their bathing suits, and at the end of the runways, before they turned and rode back, she let him kiss her on the lips and touch her breasts with his hands.

He slows down, in part because of the ice and snow and in larger part because of his reluctance to arrive at his destination. The prisoner of a past that he is unable either to accept or reject. But, then, how can anyone reject the past? Or, for that matter, accept it? There pops into his head Thomas Carlyle's comment when he was told that Margaret Fuller had decided to accept the universe: "Gad! She'd better!" And, inwardly, he laughs at himself, this Kevin O'Brien, as he has often done before, reflecting that perhaps, in the final analysis, the most anyone can expect from life is to be granted the ability to contemplate without bitterness one's own essential absurdity.

Reaching the imaginary border between Lockhartville and the neighbouring village of Frenchman's Cross—again not a real village but merely the houses along a particular short stretch of road—he discovers that someone has bought the old Dominion Atlantic Railway station, moved it away from the tracks and converted it into a house. It makes quite an ordinary-looking cottage except that the new owner, while obviously having done a good deal of competent carpentry on it, has not bothered to repaint it, so that the wall facing the road still bears the words, "Lockhartville D A R," in letters about a foot high. Kevin smiles, doubly amused because he knows that no one in Lockhartville would find that funny. They would think it stranger if a man covered a perfectly sound coat of paint merely to obliterate a sign. So the sign would stay where it was until the paint began to peel. Once when he was a child Kevin remarked to his father how odd it was that when the snow melted in the spring it uncovered the previous fall's dead leaves. His father glared at him as he always did when he said something the man considered unutterably stupid. "Where in hell else did you expect them to be?" he growled. It was a good question. Where in hell else had he expected them to be? But even now the fact struck him as odd.

One of the most memorable things that happened to him when he was a little child was the time when he and his Uncle Kaye were caught outside the locked railway station during a cloudburst—they had gone there and found the agent absent—and they crawled under a boxcar, that stood on the siding, and stayed there until it stopped raining. That was magnificent. Not that Kevin would have minded in the least getting wet. Even as an adult he was amused and a little baffled by the way most persons ran for cover as soon as they felt a few drops of rain. But he had been taught that railway cars were among the most dangerous objects in the world, and there he was hiding under one from another danger that from his point of view was entirely fictitious. The paradox enchanted him. Besides, it seemed to him then such an adult, masculine thing to do, especially in the company of the uncle who was at that time his great hero.

Kaye was a hunter, and a collector of rifles, shotguns and

pistols. During Kevin's earliest boyhood Kaye frequently spent an hour or more on a summer Sunday afternoon sitting in the privy with the door open and a .22 calibre pistol in his hand. At intervals he fired a shot at one of the wooden pins on the clothesline. He rarely missed, and then generally because of the wind. One of Kevin's first ambitions was to grow up and emulate him. When anyone asked him in those days what he wanted to be when he became a man his usual answer was "a sailor," but if he had been free to speak the truth he would have said, "I want to be a man who spends his Sunday afternoons sitting in the privy with the door open and shooting pins off the clothesline, like my Uncle Kaye."

Kaye had died in 1958 in the Springhill mine disaster, and whatever was left of his body lay entombed two miles underground. It had been the great regret of his life that he was too young for the First World War, and too old for the Second.

Kevin puts a cigarette in his mouth and pushes in the lighter on the dashboard. It is snowing much harder now. He switches on the headlights, finds they make matters worse instead of better, switches them off, and turns on the parking lights for the benefit of anyone approaching or overtaking him through the storm.

The war, he thinks, the war was so much a part of it. . . .

"What will we do with Hitler?" Miss Noseworthy asked the thirty-five children assembled in the Lockhartville school one morning in 1944. "Certainly every patriotic Canadian will agree that he must be punished as no man has ever been punished before." She made a little cage of her long, chalky-white fingers. "He could be burned at the stake, of course, roasted alive over a slow fire—but that would be too quick a death. Personally, I think he should be put in a cage like the animal he is and taken all over the world, and I'd make him eat a piece of his own body every day—a finger one day, an eyeball the next, then a slice from his leg and after that a bit of his nose—until he begged for death, blubbered like a baby, and begged to be put out of his misery." She smiled, displaying unnaturally white false teeth. "But I'd appoint the greatest doctors on earth to make sure that he didn't die."

Kevin Michael O'Brien, lieutenant of Junior Commandos, younger brother of Patrick Sean O'Brien, sergeant in the King's Own Nova Scotia Highlanders, chewed cautiously on his Juicy Fruit gum and scratched his left buttock through a hole in the hip pocket of his green corduroy pants. A few days earlier he had heard Miss Noseworthy propose that Hitler, Goering, Goebbels and Himmler be ground into sausage meat and fed to pigs. But wouldn't that be cannibalism? Pigs eating sausages? He squinted and gritted his teeth to hold back the laughter that threatened to burst, weirdly, from his mouth and nostrils.

"I'll read you a story," Miss Noseworthy told the children, who ranged in age from five to twelve and were divided into six grades. She took a magazine from the top of her desk, which also held a hardwood pointer, a bottle of Waterman's blue-black ink, a fountain pen, a large green-covered attendance register, a hand-bell and a leather strap. The magazine appeared to be *Liberty*, from a recent issue of which Kevin had torn an article telling how to recognize the difference between a Chinaman and a Jap. The Japs were hairier, he remembered, and because they wore sandals had wider spaces between their toes.

"On second thought, I won't read it," Miss Noseworthy said, putting down the magazine and curling a wisp of faded red hair around her index finger. "I'll just tell you about it. It's a wonderful story, one of the best I've ever read. Is everyone paying attention?" Her green eyes swept the room like a searchlight. "What about you, Cranston? And you, O'Brien?"

"We're paying attention, Miss Noseworthy," the boys

chanted in unison in the tone of amused but obedient altar boys responding to a slightly comic but extremely humourless priest.

"A great story," Miss Noseworthy repeated. "As good as anything ever composed by Shakespeare or Tennyson. It takes place in a Dutch village after the war. It's a story people living in Holland tell one another in whispers because if the Nazis heard them telling it they'd torture and kill them, perhaps crucify them the way they did our Canadian soldiers when they took them prisoner during the First World War, maybe cut off their hands the way they did to the Belgian babies. You're too young to know about that, you children, but I was about your age then and I remember. It happens in a Dutch village after the war when the United Nations have decided how Hitler must die."

She curled and uncurled the wisp of hair, made and unmade cages with her fingers. "He has been tied to a stake and there are kegs of gunpowder all around him. The stake has been set up in the centre of the village square and there are thousands of people there, tens of thousands, hundreds of thousands, all waiting to see him die. But the point is this: the fuse is hundreds of miles long, hundreds and hundreds of miles long; it runs through villages and towns and cities so that the people can watch the spark as it travels toward Hitler who, coward that he is, is gibbering and bawling and howling. . . . But listen to this! This is the whole point of the story, so listen very carefully. The spark finally comes close to the gunpowder, almost close enough to set it off, and old Mr. Hitler is screaming as loud as ever he can when—listen now, this is the important part—a man runs out of the crowd and stamps it out. He stamps the spark out with his feet!"

Thirty-five children exhaled. Make her stop there, Kevin said silently and to no one in particular. I want it to end there. This is important: Make her stop.

Miss Noseworthy laughed. "Well, of course that big crowd of hundreds of thousands of people wanted to kill

9

the man who had stamped out the spark. They wanted to tear him apart. You can just imagine how they shouted at him and shook their fists and some of them grabbed him and were going to kill him, right there and then. 'Why did you do it?' they kept asking him. 'Why, oh why, did you do it?' And you know what the man told them? You know what he said?" She paused, letting the tension heighten. "He said, 'I want you to do it all again.' That's what he said. 'I want you to do it all again.' "

There was loud applause from Greta Longfield who had on several occasions been told by Miss Noseworthy that she looked exactly like the child film star Margaret O'Brien. Miss Noseworthy gave a little smiling bob of the head, in what all but the smallest children knew was only feigned self-mockery. So everyone applauded, even little Billy Austin who, afterwards, as Kevin was opening his copy of *The Story of Britain and Canada,* asked, sucking the mucus up into his nose, why the man had wanted them to do it again.

As he gazed at a map that purported to show how land was divided between nobles and serfs under the feudal system, Kevin heard a train rumbling between Truro and Halifax. Its whistle sounded as it approached the crossing about three hundred yards from the school and sounded again, less urgently because it was more distant, before stopping at the airport station.

He wished he were outdoors, standing in the tall grass and dandelions beside the track, where he could see if it were one of the troop trains that carried soldiers to Windsor; they encamped there while awaiting the arrival in Halifax of the ships that would take them to Europe. The soldiers hung out of the windows of such trains, laughing and waving their caps—wedge hats, Glengarry and Balmoral bonnets, maroon, black or khaki berets.

At the apple blossom festival in Kentville where young men and women drank beer and cider and raided orchards, breaking off small branches hung with pinkish-white, sweet-smelling blossoms which they waved from the

windows of their cars, a drunken soldier had given his
wedge hat to Kevin's sister, Stephanie. Kevin had discovered that such hats had flaps which could be taken
down and buttoned under the chin, like the flaps of an
aviator's helmet. He liked to put on the hat in front of the
mirror in his bedroom, or simply take it in his hands and
run his palms back and forth over the rough cloth.

His brother, Patrick, in Italy, wore a Glengarry bonnet
with blue ribbons. Strange, Kevin reflected, that soldiers
often wore hats that looked as if they had been designed
for girls. On his last leave, Patrick had worn the Glengarry and a kilt, pretending to think the kilt a bit ridiculous
but obviously proud of it, looking very self-assured, even
a little cocky, as he strode round the village, his kilt
swinging around his strong, hairy legs, his conversation
full of knowing references to Toronto and Montreal, and
of many strange expressions picked up at the training camp
in Ontario.

"By Jesus and what are we coming to at all?" Granddad
had snorted. "An Irishman dressed up like a bloody Jock
going off to fight for a black-arsed usurping whore of a
Hanoverian king!"

The point of a pencil pricked the back of Kevin's neck.
He looked up and saw that Miss Noseworthy was facing
a blackboard, and half turned to take a scrap of paper
from the boy sitting behind him. *Buxton says he wants to
join*, the note read. Kevin hesitated, then glanced across
at Ross Cranston and nodded. He wadded the note into a
ball smaller than a marble, thinking at first that he would
catapult it with his thumb and index finger at Greta
Longfield's head, then deciding he wouldn't.

Ross was captain of the Junior Commandos, an organization fostered by the *Little Orphan Annie* radio serial, in
which Annie, her billionaire guardian Daddy Warbucks,
and his faithful retainers, Punjab and The Asp, outfought
grunting Nazis and hissing Japs. By mailing a cereal box-
top, a stamped self-addressed envelope and twenty-five
cents in stamps or coins to the radio station, you could

11

obtain a membership card, a secret decoder dial and—this was what mattered—a cardboard facsimile of a fighter plane's instrument panel with a sheet of instructions that, according to Little Orphan Annie, would teach you how to fly a Spitfire or a Hurricane.

At first the Lockhartville Junior Commandos had concentrated on searching for spies and identifying airplanes. Once they had astonished old Hymie Levinksy (who had driven through the village once a month for almost as long as anyone could remember selling clothing from door to door off the back of a truck) by running after him chanting, "Nazi! Nazi! Nazi!" But spies had to be strangers and almost the only strangers who came to Lockhartville were fliers: Canadians, Australians, Norwegians, Poles and Englishmen stationed at the RCAF Flying Training School. The presence of the air base also made plane spotting uninteresting since, although the sky was full of planes, they were virtually all unexciting little yellow biplanes called Fleets. Despite weekly blackout drills, announced by the howl of an air-raid siren, only the oldest women and smallest boys still expected someday to look up and see planes with swastikas painted on their wings.

So now the Junior Commandos mostly played at war with toy pistols and rifles, made from wood because there was a war on and now only real guns were made of metal.

Miss Noseworthy was giving the kindergarten class their reading lesson. "Here I am. My name is Nan. I have a dog. I have a cat too." The Grade 3 and 4 pupils were bent over their mud-coloured arithmetic books. Kevin filled a page in his orange Bearcat exercise book with answers to questions Miss Noseworthy had chalked on the blackboard behind her desk.

King Richard was called Richard the Lion-Hearted because he was very brave, he wrote. *He went on Crusades because he wanted to free the Holy Land from the people who did not believe in Christ.* He thought for a moment, erased the last seven words and wrote *Moslems.*

Chris Robinson nudged him and Kevin moved the exercise book slightly to the left. "Just don't copy every damn word like the last time," he whispered. "Change it around a little or old Nosey will have a haemorrhage."

King Richard was killed by an archer. The archer was skinned alive. King Richard's brother was the wicked King John. Granddad says our ancestors were kings in Ireland. O'Brien means descendant of Brian. Brian Boru. In Irish O'Brien is O'Broin. I don't remember what Kevin is, but it's Irish, too. When Brian Boru was an old man a Viking came into his tent and killed him with an axe. If the Nazis came here, I wonder if they'd kill my grandfather.

If the Nazis won the war, Kevin's father said, they would carve up Canada like a pie. He always used the same words: They would carve up Canada like a pie. The Japs would take British Columbia and possibly Alberta; perhaps the Italians would take Quebec, and the Germans would take the rest. Like carving up a pie. Perhaps Judd had read that somewhere. He read very little and remembered almost every word that he read. He also said the Bible predicted the Chinese would rule the world. And he said God made a war whenever there were too many people.

Sometimes when he was drunk Judd sang an old marching song to the tune of "When You Wore a Tulip":

> *We wear the feather, the 85th feather,*
> *We wear it with pride and joy.*
> *That fake advertiser, old Billy the Kaiser,*
> *Will hear from the Bluenose boys!*
> *His troubles are brewing, our bit we'll be*
> *doing*
> *To hammer down Britain's foes.*
> *With the bagpipes a-humming, the 85th's*
> *coming*
> *From the land where the maple leaf grows.*

"You're dreaming again, O'Brien," Miss Noseworthy said.

"I'm sorry," Kevin said.

"I'll sorry you, Mister, if you don't straighten up."

He had seen a film in which the Japs hanged a teacher from the flagpole in front of his school because he wouldn't take down the Stars and Stripes. He was a Filipino. The film had been shown at the air base where the village children were permitted to go to the movies free twice a week. He wished now, as he had wished many times before, that a dozen Jap soldiers, led by an officer with a Samurai sword, would parachute into Lockhartville and hang Miss Noseworthy.

Noon came.

Kevin and Ross rode their bicycles home to dinner, their pant-legs rolled up almost to their knees to keep them from catching in the chains. It was a hot day and they took off their shirts and tied them around their waists like sashes so that as they pedalled the empty sleeves streamed out behind them.

"Old Buxton's scared skinny," Ross reported cheerfully. "He's damn near peeing his pants."

"You sure he'll keep his trap shut? The little son of a bitch has a tongue a yard long."

"You starting to turn chicken?"

"Hell, no. I'm just saying Buxton talks too much."

"Race you to your place," Ross shouted. "Last one there is an old cow's arse in flytime."

Then they were off, bent low over the handlebars, buttocks lifted from their saddles, all their weight thrown against the whirling pedals, the loose gravel spraying out from beneath the rear wheels like machine-gun bullets. They rode past the yellow and brown airport station, not much larger than a woodshed. Past the sawmill, with its soaring smokestack and screaming saws, the great yellow oxen in their bright red yokes, muzzles almost touching the ground, hauling sledges loaded with logs tied together with chains—the teamster walking in front of them, the handle of his whip resting on his shoulder, the lash swaying back and forth almost gently behind him. Past the railway siding on which sat the huge mysterious boxcars that would carry the lumber to Halifax.

14

And in the sky as always the yellow biplanes swarmed, their motors droning like hornets, the sunlight glinting on the domes of their cockpits.

"There's a letter come from Patrick," his Aunt Lorna said as he entered the house. "Put on your shirt before you sit down to your dinner, and wash your face and hands. Twelve years old and I can't think how you manage to get so dirty." Her face and arms were red from the heat of the stove. She had been making apple pies and there were streaks of flour and sugar on her temples where she had brushed the hair away from her eyes. "The letter's there on the table, next to the window." She wiped sweat from her face with the corner of her apron. The kitchen smelled of roast beef, oniony gravy, baked potatoes, cinnamon and tea.

The letter, like all of Patrick's letters, teased about girls and wine. *Dad, the vino here tastes worse than that home-brew of Granddad's I used to get into when I was a kid. But, boy, does it kick. Aunt Lorna, don't be surprised if your favourite nephew comes back after the war with a little Eye-tie bride.* Kevin was much more interested in the paper on which it was written, tough yet almost transparent with the words *Canadian Army Somewhere in Italy* printed under a crest at the top of each sheet, and the envelope, small, wrinkled and covered with postmarks and gray smudges, some of which were recognizable as fingerprints. He liked to touch Patrick's letters and look at them. Reading them almost always bored him.

His father and his Uncle Kaye came from the sawmill, bits of sawdust in the two or three days' growth of beard on their faces, the sharp, sweet smell of sawdust hanging about them, sawdust trickling from their sleeves as they ate. Judd O'Brien read his son's letter in silence, grunted when he finished with it and laid it back on the table.

"Well, at least we can be thankful to God the boy's alive yet," Granddad said. "What with the bloody Huns on one side of him and the bloody Limeys on the other, it's God's grace he hasn't got a bullet in his craw before

15

this, and God forgive me if he doesn't deserve it going off to fight for the bloody bastards that shot Jim Connolly and him tied to a chair, by Jesus, tied to a chair."

"Almost wish I'd of been old enough to go," Kaye said, his mouth full of buttered potato. "Too young for the first war and too old for the second." He looked across at Kevin. "Same thing's going to happen to you: too young for this one, too old for the next. You mark my words."

"Maybe there won't be any more wars," Aunt Lorna said, coming back from the stove with more gravy and potatoes.

"There'll always be wars," Judd told her. "Wars and rumours of wars. Bible says so."

"What are rumours of wars?" Kevin asked.

His father put down his fork and looked at him in disgust. "You don't know what rumours of wars means? And you twelve years old. Honest to God, there's times I think I made a half-wit when I made that one. Him almost a man full-grown and he don't know what rumours of wars is."

"Stop asking questions and eat your dinner, Kevin," Aunt Lorna said, her eyes denying the anger in her voice.

"It's right there in the Bible," Judd insisted, rather sulkily.

After dinner, Kevin read the latest instalment of Buck Rogers in the *Star Weekly*. The Second World War had ended five hundred years earlier with the extermination of the Japs, except for a handful who had escaped by spaceship to a distant planet. Now the descendants of those escapees had determined to conquer the universe. And Buck Rogers was piloting the ultimate weapon, 99-Zero, toward the Planet Nippon, a weapon that was part spaceship, part bullet and part bomb, a weapon that would blow up the planet with its little yellow, slant-eyed, buck-toothed, bow-legged inhabitants. Shaped like a bullet, silver and blue, every week 99-Zero came nearer its target.

Here was something far more real than Patrick's letters: the reality of nightmare which was so often more real than the reality of everyday life. It was possible to ignore the daytime realities, leave them in the outer circles of con-

16

sciousness; but nightmares forced themselves into the very core of the mind.

He went upstairs to his room, took off his sneakers, slightly smelly socks, shirt and pants, and lay on his bed in his undershorts. It was very hot.

He began the game or, rather, let it begin, for it had a life of its own. To play the game he lay almost perfectly still while his consciousness melded with the hot, throbbing excitement of his body. He shut his eyes so tightly his ears rang, and clenched his teeth as though in pain.

Soon he was not only himself, but another: the Conqueror.

The Conqueror was standing amongst his paladins in a vast room with pillars and chandeliers. On a table with a marble top there lay spread out a map of the country which he, the Conqueror, had lately defeated.

"This province we will annex," said the Conqueror, marking off a large section of the map with a gold pencil. "Its population will be dispersed through the Empire as slaves."

Kevin moistened his lips. His buttocks rocked gently. The Conqueror marked off another province. "This area," he announced, "will be made a protectorate. The few cities it possesses will be levelled and it will be made a country of farms whose fields and herds will provide us with food and leather. Fortunately, a large part of the adult population is illiterate. We will make it an offence, punishable by death, to teach a child to read and write. Within fifty years these people will be as ignorant and content as their livestock. It will be a nation of human cows."

He was sweating now; his armpits and groin were moist, his face burning. The Conqueror continued his monologue.

"Citizens of the empire will be sent to the protectorate as landlords and overseers. There will be plantations like those which once existed in the southern United States. Such plantations will be awarded to officers who have shown great courage."

The Conqueror gestured toward the last and smallest section of the map. "We will permit this region to remain

17

independent, a country where the land is barely fertile enough to support human life. I see it as a country of hungry outlaws, too small and weak to endanger our security and yet large enough to keep our frontier guards alert and to provide a useful buffer against the empire of the east. From time to time, of course, we will mount small expeditions against the outlaws—an excellent method of keeping our soldiers in fighting trim."

The Conqueror gestured again and an aide quickly folded up the map. The generals, admirals and cabinet ministers waited for some sign that they were dismissed. "There is one more matter," said the Conqueror. "The slaves must be taught to walk about naked, like animals. . . ." At this point Kevin began trembling violently.

"Kevin!" Aunt Lorna shouted from the hall below. "Hurry on down here! You'll be late for school again."

After a moment the boy dressed hurriedly and ran downstairs.

The headquarters of the Junior Commandos was a government gravel pit about a half-mile from the main road. It had been a wet summer and a pool deep enough to float a raft carrying four or five boys had formed like a miniature lake at the bottom of the pit. There was a wooden tower, about thirty feet tall, built for weighing gravel, from the top of which one could see, over the trees and across the river, the black roof of a hangar, and the high flapping sleeve that showed the pilots the direction of the wind. Trees grew around the rim of the pit, so much of the earth beneath them dug away that their roots were exposed like great petrified subterranean spiders. There was a toolshed which the boys used as a clubhouse, having learned that the padlock on its door could be unscrewed with a jackknife and hammered back into place with a few blows from a stone.

The boys, six of them, gathered there after school, waiting for Buxton.

"Bet a dollar the bastard doesn't show up," Lee Alton said, lighting a handmade cigarette with a kitchen match.

"I'll be a hell of a lot happier if he don't," Keith

Anderson said. "We must be getting damn hard up for members when we have to take that little jerk."

"He'll be here all right," Ross Cranston said, rubbing his thumb and forefinger together under Lee's nose to show he wanted a drag off his cigarette.

"He'll be here," Kevin agreed. He had been made a lieutenant by Cranston not because he was a leader among the boys but because his reading of newspapers and magazines had earned him a certain respect as an authority on military jargon.

A few minutes later, Buxton appeared, a boy of ten, almost cross-eyed with fear.

"Hi, there, fellas," he said, his voice quavering so that all of them laughed.

"Hello, Stupid," Alton sneered.

"Shut up, Alton," Ross said.

"Yes, sir," Alton said, half in mockery, half in grudging respect.

Ross walked around Buxton, like a man examining a piece of dubious merchandise. The others waited, grinning, except for Kevin whose face was expressionless.

"So you want to become a Commando?" Ross said at last.

"Yeah, sure, yeah," Buxton said, scuffing his sneakers in the gravel.

"Say 'Yes, sir,' when you answer the captain," Kevin said, his tone so amiable that Buxton almost smiled.

"Yes, sir," said Buxton cheerfully.

"You know what you are?" Ross snarled, bringing his face very close to Buxton's. "You're a chickenshit Nazi spy, that's what you are."

"You tell the bastard," Alton said.

"Shut up, Alton," Ross said. "I'm not going to tell you again. Shut your goddamn mouth, you hear me?"

"Yes, sir," Alton said.

"That goes for the rest of you, too. We're going to see that this thing is done right this time."

"You, Alton, and you, Simpson, blindfold this spy," Ross said.

Buxton stood white-faced and giggling as he was blind-folded with a dirty red and white handkerchief.

"Now march him over to the interrogation room."

"Huh?" said Simpson.

"The clubhouse, you jerk. Can't you remember any-thing?"

Buxton was led to the toolshed; the padlock was removed and he was taken inside.

"Now tie the damn spy up," Ross ordered, "and make sure you tie him good and tight."

Buxton's hands were tied together in front of him with a length of grocer's cord. The free end of the cord was thrown over a beam and secured. He stood with his arms outstretched above him, his toes barely touching the floor. "Let's kill him right here and now and get it over with," Simpson said.

"Naw, that would be too quick," Alton said. "I want to see the son of a bitch squirm a little."

"What is this, fellas?" Buxton asked, fear muffling his voice like a cloth over his face. He twisted his head, trying to see around the edges of the blindfold.

"Get the light bulb, Alton," Ross said.

"What are you gonna do to me?" Buxton quavered.

Alton pressed the hot bulb hard against Buxton's bare chest and held it there.

"Give it to the kraut bastard!" the boys shouted. "Burn him good."

Buxton squirmed and tried to pull away, whimpering.

"Listen to the yellow bastard beg!" Alton yelled.

"Say 'Heil Hitler!' you Nazi arsehole," Simpson ordered.

"Say it! Say it! Make him say it!" the others chorused.

"You better say it," Kevin said, as Cranston handed Alton a fresh bulb.

"I'll say it," Buxton whined. "Just stop burning me. I'll say it."

"Say it, then," Alton said. "Say it," and he exerted all his strength, pressing the hot glass against Buxton's skin.

"Heil Hitler!"

20

"Louder!"

"Heil Hitler!"

"Louder!"

"Heil Hitler!"

"I guess that's all the proof we need," Ross said. "Let's take him out and kill him."

"You want us to kill you?" Alton demanded. "You want us to hang you up by the neck, you goddamn Nazi?"

"No," Buxton breathed. "Just let me go home. I wanta go home. Just let me go home."

"We're going to be real good to you," Ross told him. "We're going to give you a second chance."

The bulb had cooled. Alton carefully returned it to its socket. Kevin was sweating almost as much as Buxton, and his hands were trembling.

"Yeah, give him a second chance," agreed the others.

"You still want to be a Commando?" Ross asked.

"Yeah," Buxton said. "Yeah, I guess so."

"Okay. Well, all you got to do is this. You got to do anything that any of us tells you to do for a week. You got that?"

"Yeah, I guess so. Only can't you untie me now?"

"If one of us tells you to eat cowshit, you'll eat cowshit. You got that?"

"Yeah."

"Say 'Yes, sir,' when you talk to the captain," Alton said. "Or you'll get burnt again."

"Yes, sir."

"Okay, then. But don't forget what I told you," Cranston said. "You do everything you're told to do for a week and maybe we'll let you be a Commando. I said 'maybe.' Go ahead, Simpson, untie him."

Buxton was untied. The blindfold was removed. He looked about him, almost hysterical with relief.

"I guess a guy's gotta go through a lotta tests before he gets into this club?" he said, grinning, although his eyes still showed the depths of his terror.

"He's beginning to get the idea," Alton said.

21

"He's a real smart kid," Ross said. "He learns fast."

"You run along home now," Simpson said. "Before we decide we was too easy on you."

"Yeah, you better go home," Kevin said.

"But don't forget what I told you," Ross said. "You got to do everything we tell you to do for a week."

"I won't forget," Buxton said. "I won't forget, sir."

He turned and ran, falling several times as he clambered up the side of the pit.

"You think he'll go through with it?" Simpson asked.

"He hasn't got the guts," Alton said.

"He hasn't got the guts not to," Kevin said. "He'll go through with it all right."

"Wait till we lower him down the side of the tower," Ross laughed. "Jesus. Can't you see his face?"

"Let's have a swim," Alton said. "God, it's hot."

And they stripped naked and swam in the pool at the bottom of the pit. But first Kevin went behind the tool-shed and vomited.

the
imaginary
soldier

And that was not the last time, Kevin reflects as he continues to drive through the falling snow, not the last time that I was an imaginary soldier.

To him, the Second World War will always be simply: "The War." He has a friend, an American of his own age, who says that for him Franklin Roosevelt was the only real president of the United States: his predecessors were myths and his successors have been impostors. Perhaps, Kevin thinks, we live the first rough drafts of our lives before we're thirteen years old and everything after that —youth, manhood, middle age, old age, senility—is a series of revised versions of the same basic text.

He has tried over the years to find the meaning of various incidents in his life and to give form to them. The briefcase that he carries with him on this trip contains a number of manuscripts in which he has attempted to explore and explain his past. But though the plot may be fixed the pattern is constantly changing. The childhood Kevin remembers at twenty-five is different from the child-hood he remembered at twenty. The childhood that he will remember should he happen to be alive twenty years from now will be something else again. Already he has watched his youth undergo its first transformation. Certain persons and places have grown in importance, while others have dissolved into insignificance and are almost forgotten. The protagonist changes too. The teenaged Kevin O'Brien that the twenty-five-year-old Kevin O'Brien remembers was piteously young for his years, whereas that person considered himself to be unusually mature; there were even times when he thought of himself as an old man. The matter is complicated further by the fact that none of these former selves will die until the final Kevin O'Brien is dead.

Most of these changes are part of something that happens to us, rather than of something that we do. But Kevin learned while he was still a child that at times it is possible for one deliberately to alter the course of events that have already taken place. What's needed is a better-than-average memory and possession of the quality most essential to professional soldiers, athletes and criminals: an unhesitating willingness to take necessary risks, coupled with the ability to distinguish immediately those risks that are unnecessary.

Then there are the memories that the brain has shaped into memoirs, those that have been mixed with oil and pressed on to the canvas with a palette knife as compared with those that float about in the mind like watercolour on moist paper. The manuscripts in his briefcase represent his attempts to create such memoirs.

Kevin interrupts his reveries as he stops for gasoline. A tall, thin elderly man in overalls and a cloth cap comes out to work the pump. His facial expression goes through a rapid succession of changes as he looks more and more closely at the young man behind the steering wheel. His eyes are at first startled, then curious, then self-satisfied. Bending close to the open car window he says, "You know who this is, don't you?"

"Sure," Kevin answers after a moment's hesitation. If he admits that he cannot recall ever having seen the man before he will not be believed; it will be assumed that having moved to a city and found a job where he does not get his hands dirty he is playing the traitor to his origins. Yet he has to appear to be a bit hesitant, otherwise they— the villagers, all of whom will sooner or later be given an account of this meeting—will wonder why he did not give some sign of recognition the moment that he stopped.

"Me and the wife was talkin' about you just the other day. We read that piece you wrote in *Maclean's*. The wife tore it out and sent it to Ross. He's in Boston now, but more than likely you knew that. He's got a real good job down there."

24

So this is Ross Cranston's father, Kevin thinks. How odd to meet as an adult someone you remember as having been an adult when you were still a child; how strange to be expected to greet as an old friend, or at the very least as an old acquaintance, someone who is actually a total stranger. "No, I didn't know. I've been sort of out of touch," Kevin says.

"Him and his wife they've got three kids now. Two boys and a girl. You married yet?" Kevin shakes his head. The other laughs. "Well, like they say, it's foolish to buy a cow when you can get your milk for nothin'. The next time the wife writes to Ross, I'll make sure she tells him I seen you."

"That's great," Kevin says. Nothing is lonelier than a service station at dusk except perhaps a bus station after midnight. "I suppose he married Rodney MacTavish's daughter, the one with the funny name."

"What?" Ross Cranston's father grins meekly for an instant, like a very polite man who suspects that he has missed the point of what ought to have been a very simple joke. "Oh, that one. Annie Laurie MacTavish, you mean. No, he married a girl from Boston. A Portuguese girl, she is. Sure sounds funny to the wife and me to hear our grandchildren spittin' out the Portuguese to one another and them no bigger than a fart in a mitten. Still, the way me and the wife look at it, it would of been worse if she'd of been French. The Portuguese know their place; you can say that much for them." There is a momentary silence. "How about the oil? Is it okay or do you want I should check it for you?"

"No, thanks." Kevin reaches for the handle that raises the window. The service station possesses what is almost certainly the only neon sign in Lockhartville. "Good to see you again."

"Take care."

"Right. Be seeing you." It has stopped snowing, and Kevin has only a little farther to drive. He will smoke at least two more cigarettes and make a brief stop, parking at the mouth of a logging road long enough to drink deeply from a flask of rum, and to urinate. (As a very small boy it disturbed him that the characters in comic strips—Tim Tyler and Bud Bartlett, for instance, of the Ivory Patrol—never were known to poop or pee.) He will also think about Ross Cranston, Lee Alton, and the other Junior Commandos. And his mind will turn to one of the manuscripts in his briefcase, a fragment of autobiography:

My first real glimpse of the great world outside our village was in a photograph, or it may have been a cartoon, in a newspaper. (When I strive to reproduce that picture in my mind's eye I see Picasso's *Guernica* instead. I try to push aside the Picasso, because it's as if the picture I want to see were concealed behind it, but I never succeed: the Picasso won't move. The newspaper may even have published a reproduction of the painting, although that's improbable; it's much more likely to have been a rough pen and ink sketch like those on the editorial page of the New York *Daily News*.) I looked at it for what must have been a very long time and with a feeling that I can only describe as awe—awe in an ancient, elemental sense. When I took it to my father and asked him what it meant, he said, "Spain." At least I don't remember him saying more than that: for small children an incomprehensible answer is often enough; they merely want to be assured that an answer exists. But it's possible he also told me that men were fighting in Spain, and that the picture depicted the results of a bombing raid. The Spanish Civil War began when I was three and a half and ended when I was six years and one month old.

So I was still a child, a twelve-year-old boy, when Hitler's war ended, and I lived in Nova Scotia, separated by an ocean from the fighting. There are witnesses. Not that they would remember me, for none of them ever knew me, but they would remember a boy named Kevin

O'Brien. Common sense says I was that boy and nobody else. But, then, common sense is no more than what its name suggests: a consensus. Years later there was a time when I came dangerously close to separating into two persons: a drunken Kevin wrote letters to a sober Kevin beginning, *You poor sick sober dunderhead,* and the sober Kevin tore them up.

Even now, after more than a quarter of a century, I have dreams in which I'm a soldier in the Second World War. I've also dreamt of being Alexander I, Czar of Russia, as he rode in triumph through villages recaptured from the armies of Napoleon, with the people cheering him and throwing flowers under the hooves of his horse. And I once dreamt that I was presented to Hitler at the 1936 Olympics in Berlin, which, if nothing else, illustrates how the rational mind can give form to the subconscious. Then there were the dreams, a series of them, in which I was a guard at Nuremberg and may have smuggled cyanide to Goering. Not that any of these dreams were as orderly as I may have seemed to suggest. In the Goering dreams there was a great green meadow in which I met his wife and daughter, but the important thing that happened there was that a huge white goat jumped up on me like a dog and pounded my chest and shoulders with his hooves—whereupon I saw a friend from the years when I worked for the Hainesville *Weekly Advertiser.* He sat on a stone or a log and he wore a red shirt. This was the one time that I know for a certainty that I dreamt in colour, for within the dream I carefully registered the fact that his shirt was red. We talked, and he said that when two persons met as he and I were meeting it meant that they were both of them dreaming the same dream.

"You've made an important discovery," I said (I was extremely excited about it), "I must telephone you in the morning and confirm this."

"You'd be wasting your time," he said, "I never remember my dreams."

I'm standing in a corridor in what is evidently a prison. I know that I'm not a prisoner because there's a pistol

strapped to my hip. I wear battledress and am facing a
steel door in which there's an opening, smaller than a
window and somewhat larger than the usual peephole,
covered with either steel bars or mesh, I'm not certain
which. The corridor is lined with such doors, and with
soldiers. We stand at ease, but formally, legs apart and
hands behind our backs, neither looking at one another nor
speaking. Facing me from the other side of the steel door,
his head framed by the barred or mesh-covered opening as
though in a satirical portrait, is Goering.

He resembles a Dickensian Fat Boy, and I'm reminded of
such a boy whom I knew in Grade 5, Neddie Gallope, who
consumed Crackerjack in vast quantities, and giggled.
True to the Dickensian tradition, the teacher enjoyed beating him. This became so obvious that two or three of the
boys informed on him repeatedly for minor violations of
the rules, not from dislike (they were his particular cronies,
as a matter of fact), but out of a craving to be entertained.
They were diverted not so much by his pain, which wasn't
severe, as by the evident enthusiasm with which the
teacher inflicted it. Afterwards he would bluster at them,
his fat cheeks red and sweaty, but it seemed he was more
scandalized than resentful; and it was never long before
they had him laughing with them.

Goering talks. I wish I could tell you what he says, but
I'm not at all sure that I'm listening. Perhaps he's reciting
the story of his life, about which I know little. He was a
pilot, a gourmand, a codeine addict, a looter of paintings;
he built a castle where he hunted wild boar and played
with electric trains. Once—was it in conversation with
Goebbels?—he joked about Jews having snouts like caribou.
That's about as much as I know about him, awake or
asleep.

I sense that he despises me, carelessly, languidly, as
arrogant men often despise those from whom they have
little or nothing to fear—their contempt so wholehearted
that it's almost gentle, and might even, under certain circumstances, be mistaken for rough affection. It's plain that
he knows that I'm nobody and will continue to be nobody

even if it should happen to be me that knots the rope under his ear and releases the trap.

I don't doubt that he deserves to die. But his death, and the manner of it, needn't concern me. I know, like everybody else, that none of these prisoners will escape. Already we've read their last words and heard the legend that their ashes were dumped into garbage cans or flushed down a sewer. So even as I stand here I know for a certainty that Goering will not be hanged, that he will take poison, although they—we?—will lay his body with the others beside the gallows. Everything happening here is part of the past, which makes me simultaneously powerless and free.

In this dream I hail from Akron, Ohio. I can't say whether I know more about Akron now than when I'm awake, because there is no reason for anyone to question me about it. Neither can I be sure that I know my own name, since nobody asks it. But none of this bothers me as it would if I weren't asleep.

Then I'm somewhere else: in a Bavarian meadow.

"It's little enough that we're asking," a young girl is saying to me. She is Goering's daughter. "We're not asking you to let him escape," she says, "just to allow him to die in his own way." The wife is there, also, but she doesn't speak and I think, although I'm not sure of this, that she's invisible.

Then comes the goat that pounds me with its hooves. "Get it away from me," I plead. A woman laughs.

Many of my war dreams are fearful, particularly those involving air raids, in which, incidentally, I'm always on the ground, and never among the attackers. Sometimes after the bombs fall the sky changes colour, turns purple, green, or red, and I know that the world is about to end. Afterwards I sit half-awake on the side of the bed and smoke a cigarette or thumb through an innocuous book, unwilling to fall asleep again for fear that, as has sometimes happened, the nightmare will resume. A very few of the dreams are merely entertaining; I was reminded of them when I stood in the replica of the cockpit of Nelson's

Victory in Madame Tussaud's amidst the smell of artificial gunsmoke and the roar of imaginary cannon.

The dreams come, in one form or another, only once or twice a year; they're notable not for their frequency but for their persistence: I've been having them almost all of my life.

I'm a veteran who has never gone to war, and there must be many of us. I have a friend, several years older than I am, who describes the Normandy invasion so subjectively and with such verisimilitude that for a long time I assumed he had participated in it. Eventually I learned that when the fighting stopped he was still in high school in Canada. He says he reads books about the war only because detective stories bore him. But I strongly suspect that he, too, belongs to the Legion of Imaginary Soldiers, and has driven a Bren gun carrier in his sleep.

"God bless Mummy. God bless Daddy. God bless everybody. Except the Germans. Amen." Once when I was six I ended my bedtime prayer with those words, causing my mother to laugh at me, lovingly, not only then but each time she retold the story—which is what I had intended, for I felt no malice toward the Germans, but only wanted to please.

The day of Pearl Harbor I was confused and perhaps even annoyed that as I listened to Jack Benny on the radio the program was continually broken into by news bulletins about warplanes with the rising sun on their wings. I supposed that meant the glare of reflected sunlight had kept them from being identified. I'd never heard of the Japanese.

A few years ago I ran into a man who, on learning where I was born, said that he'd been stationed there during the war, at the RCAF Flying Training School that, as I told him, was within sight of our house. At least from our dooryard we could see the gatehouse and the roof of the hangar, with its observation tower, searchlight, wind-sleeve and flagstaff. It was odd, talking with him, his Lockhartville being so different from mine. I wondered if

30

we'd ever seen each other there, perhaps at the Contact Inn, a barn of a place, of which it was said without a deal of exaggeration that it had been thrown up the day the flying school opened and would be torn down the day that it closed. There was a little hole-in-the-wall store in front, where Jimmy Wavell, the owner and the kind of unabashed and dissolute old entrepreneur who ends up cheerfully hawking potato peelers at country fairs, sold light groceries, candy, soft drinks and ice cream. All of the kids went there. Most of the remainder of the ground floor was taken up by a single large room containing a piano and a few tables and chairs, and with Japanese lanterns and red, white, and blue crepe paper streamers hanging from the ceiling: a sort of makeshift night club. The second storey was much smaller than the first, a kind of penthouse, where Wavell lived and where there were two or three bedrooms that could be rented by the airmen by the day or the hour. "The things that happened there!" the former pilot said, liking me because I'd provided him with an excuse for remembering. "God, there was this girl from the village, this big blonde, and one night upstairs at old Jimmy's we. . . ." He laughed so often and so hard, telling his story, that I wouldn't have been sure what the joke was, even if I'd been attentive, which I wasn't; I was reflecting on the possibility that the big blonde he'd taken upstairs was my mother.

My memories of my mother are so sparse that when I was a child and a young man there was an empty place in my past which I attempted to fill with a succession of almost wholly imaginary women with little in common other than that for nine months each of them had held me in her womb. At first these women were created by others. "That bitch you married," Aunt Lorna would say to my father when he came home surly and smelling of rum, and swore at the doors or kicked the furniture as though they, simply by being part of the physical world, were involved in the cosmic conspiracy against him. Always when Lorna was angry at my father she would call up my mother's ghost and curse it, her eyes unnaturally alert, her canine teeth bared. "Fried green tomatoes!" she would sneer, or something that would have sounded equally inconsequential to a listener unfamiliar with the canon of her inculpations. Years before, it seemed, his young wife had fried green tomatoes (Lorna would as soon have made a stew from angleworms), and he—the sap—had eaten them. Yes, and more than once, Lorna had seen him with her own eyes and nobody else's, sitting on that very couch— and as she pointed to it, his eyes obeyed her—with that stinking bitch, that cow, all over him, her legs every which way, while he squeezed a pimple on the back of her neck. "That was enough to make a dog throw up," she said, "if anything was."

Without ever saying so in words she was certain I'd understand, she made it clear that she doubted that I was my father's son. "That one," she said, "Charlie Butler will never be dead as long as he's alive." And had he heard the joke, she wanted to know, that was told by the fliers? One of them, after lying with the whore on the riverbank, in the mud, like a sow, had asked her price and been told it was a package of cigarettes.

I was a man before I found out that elsewhere, if not in Lockhartville, fried green tomatoes were regarded as edible. I happened upon the recipe in a James Beard cookbook and, inevitably, the first chance I got I bought green tomatoes, fried them and ate them. I'm still not sure if I like them for their taste, or because of the messages they send back through time to the child that I used to be.

It's not surprising that communication between human beings is so difficult, considering that so much of what each of us feels most deeply can't help but seem the merest trivia to almost everyone else.

By the time I was fourteen or fifteen I had become more adept at selecting the materials from which to create the myth. One of the stories Aunt Lorna told was this: Leah (my mother's name), when she was an adolescent, was known to board the train at Frenchman's Cross, where she then lived, pay the conductor ten cents, ride the three miles to Lockhartville, get off there and walk home. And if that wasn't foolish enough, Lorna said, there was the way she acted while she was aboard; everybody in Lockhartville and Frenchman's Cross laughed their heads off about it. She'd ask the conductor would he fetch her a pillow, and she'd stretch out her legs and lean back, with her arms under her head and her eyes shut. Or if there was room enough she'd curl up on the seat; or maybe she'd just sit looking out the window, putting expressions on her face like she was a movie actress, yawning and stretching and trying to look bored—pretending, you see, that she'd come a long way and had a long way to go, imitating the people she'd seen who'd ridden all the way from Boston or New York to Toronto, and she, why, she'd never been farther from home than Halifax in her life.

When the war in Europe ended there were riots in Halifax. Fifty miles away in Lockhartville we didn't know about it until the following day, although having heard the radio warn residents of the city to keep off the streets, we were aware that something extraordinary was happening there. Several years later I heard a man who had witnessed the riots tell of seeing a gang of sailors strip a girl naked on the sidewalk, throw away her cheap clothing and dress her again in things they'd looted from the most expensive stores. It took them a very long time to find shoes that would fit her, he said, so that dozens of pairs they'd discarded were scattered on the pavement. The last thing they put on her was a fur coat that he assumed to be mink; and they'd found diamonds for her neck, wrists and fingers. They were just kids, he said, the sailors, and didn't hurt the girl, or mean to scare her. None of them so much as pinched her bum.

My brother Patrick, who was killed in Italy and lies buried in Rimini, is another imaginary character. "There's bad news, Kev," my father said to me. "Your brother. Patrick. He's dead." And my first reaction was pleasure that my father had called me Kev, which he did only on those rare occasions when from joy or sadness or mere forgetfulness he ceased momentarily to be afraid of me. Then I wondered what he wanted me to do. If I cried

would he regard it as a further demonstration of my gut-
lessness? If I failed to cry would he consider that additional
proof that I was selfish and unfeeling? The answer to both
questions was Yes.

"God damn the Germans," I said, unconvincingly, and
at the same moment each of us turned away.

Of course I'd loved it when Patrick came home on em-
barkation leave and we walked into the Contact Inn or
Vaughan's General Store, him in his Ladies from Hell kilt
and me wearing his Glengarry bonnet to show everyone
we belonged together. But other than that about all I
remembered of him was that once he had used the long
pole with which we drew water from the well, to pole-vault
over the fence between the backyard and the heath, and
another time he had tied me to a post at the farthest end
of the pasture and then frightened me by walking away
as if to abandon me there.

When, as happened two or three times a year, a student
or instructor from the flying school was killed in a crash,
the flag on top of the hangar was lowered to half-staff. We
always glanced expectantly in its direction as we came out
of the schoolhouse. Some of the fliers were almost madly
reckless, flying their little yellow biplanes under bridges or
so low that they returned to the airport with leaves or even
stalks of grain clinging to their landing gear. When one
of them was killed, the others, whom we'd overhear dis-
cussing his death, almost always agreed that it was largely
his own fault. That may have been only their way of
reassuring themselves, but I've since noticed that it's a
habit of old soldiers, this emphasizing of the victim's share
in the responsibility. When I asked my great-uncle, who
fought with Lord Strathcona's Horse in the South African
War, about a bronze statue of a soldier in the uniform of
that war, standing in the square in Larchmont, he said,
"They put that up for George Bailey, his family did; I was
there when he got it; it wouldn't have happened if he
hadn't been a bloody fool, and a show-off."

The medieval knights are said to have been grateful to
God for what they took to be His pledge that those who

34

lived by the sword would be privileged to die by it. If I had known when I was twelve that I was certain to die in battle before I was twenty, I'd have been happy. That was what the world was like then.

We were in school when word came that the war was over. We cheered even before Miss Noseworthy said we could take the rest of the day off. Later, when I was alone, I almost succeeded in persuading myself that it was Patrick, or my mother, or both of them, that made me weep.

life
and
times

Although electric power came to Lockhartville at the
beginning of the war, there remain two houses that have
not been wired for electricity. One belongs to Morley
Neilson, an elderly bachelor farmer who maintains that he
has never felt a need for any of the things that electricity
would provide for him. The other is Judd O'Brien's.

Judd has often talked of the day when he would have
his place wired—hardly anyone in Lockhartville uses the
expressions "home" and "house"; instead they say "place,"
with a special intonation. But each time that he has saved
enough money to pay for having the work done, something
else has turned up. There has been an emergency, or he
has celebrated by getting drunk and has woken up to find
that he has spent it.

So the light in the window of the O'Brien place is soft
and tinged with red. Kevin drives into the yard and stops
beside the well with its waist-high curb and ten-foot-long
pole. It has stopped snowing, and the stars have come out.
As he opens the door and starts to get out of the car he
smells the sea.

It is one of the curiosities of Lockhartville that while it
is near the sea it is not often that anyone goes there, since
all the roads turn inland. To reach the coast by car it's
necessary to drive forty miles or more, although as the
crow or the gull flies it is only four or five miles away.

Kevin pauses for a moment and looks at the house
which is in darkness except for what he knows to be the
kitchen. I am David Balfour arriving at the House of
Shaws, he thinks to himself, except that this house holds
no surprises for me.

There was a time when almost every room in this house

37

was a nation. He had devoted so much time during his childhood and youth to building worlds! No, that's not strictly true; he had spent most of the time doing other things, as everybody spends most of the time doing other things. God is said to have devoted only six days out of eternity to creating the universe.

The latter worlds of Kevin O'Brien's creation had been almost purely internal: visions with which he entertained himself as he waited to fall asleep. But the earlier ones had required certain physical apparatus. They were sacramental, rather than mystical.

He had made kings and queens and their soldiers and subjects, using scissors and pages torn from exercise books, and he had clothed them with crayon and housed them in palaces and fortresses made from cardboard boxes imprinted with names such as Schwartz Peanut Butter and Kraft Pure Orange Marmalade.

The kitchen had been Betagaria, the pantry Wabovia, the dining room Alpinia, separated from Betagaria by a mountain range—the wall—penetrated only by a great river, the door. The stairs had been the high seas, and the upstairs bedrooms Mosqueia, Malevia, Upalia and Whitorocco, all of these nation-states having been villages when he was younger: the Kingdom of Wabovia of his thirteenth year had been the Washboardville of his third, so-named for his grandmother's washboard, as Betagaria, a great empire rent by civil war, had been at its inception Betville, named for a doll of Stephanie's that she called Bet.

Kevin walks across the muddy yard to the house while bits of the past, the present and the future bounce about in his mind as beads of cold water bounce about in a hot frying pan.

Although it's been five years or more since we saw one another last, he'll not come out of the house nor even open the door to greet me. He'll be waiting for the sound of my car turning off the road and stopping in the backyard, a place more familiar to me than any other spot in the world will ever be, and when he hears it he'll go to the kitchen window and peer around the blind, being very careful not to be seen; but he'll be supine on the couch, perhaps with a copy of *The Ring* or *Police Gazette* or *True Detective* or *Argosy* lying open across his chest, when I knock with fraudulent jauntiness, "shave and a haircut, two bits," and he calls, "Come in."

I'll take his hand in mine and shake it, then sit down in the chair that will be standing beside the window that faces the barn, the same chair or one so like it as to make no difference in which I sat so many nights reading, by lamplight, books like Jack London's *The Star Rover* and Vardis Fisher's *In Tragic Life*; listening to the old Admiral radio whose sounds were to me like the images seen by the inhabitants of Plato's cave, the first signals to reach me from another and larger world; eating raw onion and Kam sandwiches, or holding Holly Johnston on my lap while she pulled my hair. The room, a big old-fashioned farmhouse kitchen, with countless thicknesses of linoleum on the floor and mouseholes under the sink, will be as it was when I last saw it except for one or two curious alterations or additions: the door to the pantry will be nailed shut, for instance, or the deer antlers on the wall between the door to the pantry and the door to the dining room will be painted mauve, or there will be some strange picture cut from a magazine or salvaged from a neighbour's trash-heap.

Once there was a framed portrait of a man with a shaven egg-shaped head, enormous eyebrows, an immense moustache and a hypogastric beard. A caption identified him as General Stossel who on January 1, 1905, surrendered Port Arthur to the Japanese. His telegram of apology to the Czar began: "Great Sovereign, forgive!" Presumably someone in Lockhartville long ago had admired this man sufficiently to cut his picture out of a magazine—perhaps the *Illustrated London News*—and put it in a frame. But why? And what significance could it possibly hold for my father who had erected it here? "There's a hole in the wall there," he explained when my curiosity got the better of me. "A couple of the boys was drinkin' and they got into a little argument here a month or so ago."

He'll smell of sawdust, a feral ruttish smell like that of new-mown hay. He'll wear the sneakers, jeans and T-shirt that are virtually a uniform at the sawmill now—boyish, almost childlike garments with that timeworn seediness peculiar to old men's clothes. There will be copper wire bracelets on his wrists to ward off rheumatism, and more likely than not one or more of his fingers will be bandaged with rags and grocer's twine. His wire-rimmed eyeglasses will have been patched with thread, adhesive tape or rabbit wire.

"Hot," he'll say, or "Cold," or "Wet," as the case may be.

"Yes," I'll agree. There will be a furtive silence. "How have you been?" I'll ask.

"Can't complain," he'll say. "And yourself?"

"Oh, I'm fine," I'll answer; and soon it will be as if I had been gone no longer than an hour and been no farther than Vaughan's General Store where, when I was sixteen, I bought *Famous Fantastic Mysteries, Fantastic Novels,* Neilson's almond nut chocolate bars and Sportsman cigarettes, which I smoked because no one else in the village did.

We are as shy of one another now as we were then; shyer than any strangers could be. It's as if we both of us knew that such meetings were subject to an elaborate etiquette, and were each afraid of making a fool of himself by attempting to perform the ceremonies. It's possible we'll never once address each other by name. In sentence after sentence the name will be replaced by a pause, like a row of elliptical dots.

Liquor will help: Lamb's Navy Rum with chasers of Ten Penny Ale. The fellowship of the bottle is the one club to which we both belong. We'll take the rum straight, dehydrating our mouths and throats which we'll moisten again with the beer. Perhaps we'll put some of the beer cans into a bucket and lower them into the well to chill. After we've each of us taken about nine ounces of rum we'll begin to relax. If the rum lasts long enough he may tell me that this past summer a woman has been driving over from Halifax to spend the weekends with him: "Of course, that shocked your Aunt Lorna; but, what the hell, I'm only human." And perhaps I'll try to tell him a little about what it's like to work for a daily newspaper and get annoyed with myself for telling him about interviewing the prime minister, because I'll know that he doesn't believe me any more than I believe his story about the woman and, besides, why should he care?

The last time I got drunk with my father I resolved to write and publish his biography, *The Life and Times of Judd O'Brien*. It was to be a biography in the great tradition: documented, illustrated and indexed. Yet it would be different from any book ever written. For hitherto the Judd O'Briens have left no memoirs except their bones.

Sitting drunk on the bed on which I slept as a child, smelling the stink of decades of dried sweat on the mattress, hearing hordes of mice running about in the attic, it was almost as if I were holding the printed book in my hands. It was bound in calf and the engravings were protected by sheets of tissue paper. The title was imprinted in gold. That gave me almost enough pleasure to overcome my regret at not bringing a sleeping bag or, better still, checking into a motel in Windsor. For the time being I was utterly convinced that I had discovered my life's work and would begin next day or the day after to produce it; all that I had to do was master the incantations that would make the book that I saw in my mind's eye materialize.

I laughed at myself next morning.

The best I can do when I'm sober and awake is put Judd O'Brien into a ghost story. All fictions are ghost stories, and some fictions are exorcisms.

In one of the most vivid of my infantile memories of him, I'm running away, laughing. No, in the beginning I can't have been laughing; I suspect I was blubbering. We are in the backyard, the two of us, between the house and the barn, with the long low wagonshed on one side and the heath, with its dogwood, spruce shrubs, raspberry bushes, blueberries and wintergreen on the other. I glance back, over my shoulder, and see that his face is dark. All of a sudden, I know, I'm absolutely certain, that he would take pleasure in killing me. And that amuses me, perhaps because I'm so much quicker than he. I run backwards. I pirouette. I dance. I skip. He bellows and brandishes. I laugh like a piano.

Understand: this is no game; he really and truly wants to kill me. That's what makes it so hysterically laughable. It goes on for what seems like a very long time. I'm frightened, of course, terrified. But I don't try to escape; rather, I tease him as the barn swallow appears to tease the cat that's trying to snatch it out of the air.

He is lubberly. I'm thistledown. I take greater risks; I fly closer and closer, until at last, the darkness swoops down—and scoops me up—and swallows me.

I died then.

Fee fi fo fum. I, only this minute, reminiscing, realized whom it was that Jack the Giant Killer was running from.

My father's hands resemble other men's feet: the fingers crook and fold under one another as toes do; the thumbnails are squamous and corrugated like horn. The skin is like cowhide—he can extinguish a cigarette by pinching it between his naked thumb and index finger—and is almost sure to bear long scaly gashes, fresh scars, that will be or will seem to be a quarter of an inch deep.

When I was a small child I associated the mill with my father as I associated the church building with God. This was dirt farm country, where the nearest neighbour rarely lived less than a half-mile away; a quiet place, where on Sundays the only communal sounds came from roosters, cows, dogs and children. But six days a week, from seven o'clock in the morning until six o'clock in the afternoon,

everyone in the settlement heard—couldn't help but hear
—the mill.

At a distance they were rather soothing sounds: the
engine snoring gently while the saws played Johnny-
One-Note on their tin whistles. Close at hand they were
frightening, at least to me, as thunder is frightening;
although I know that it's harmless I'm uneasy that it
speaks with such power.

Four times a day there came the wild sad scream of the
whistle, calling the men back to their jobs. The smoke and
steam that rolled up out of the sixty-foot-high stack and
drifted away toward the clouds was yellowish-blue, the
colour of bruised flesh. Even now, so many years later, I
find myself using that smokestack as a unit of measure-
ment. I read that such and such an object is three hundred
feet long and I picture it as being five times the length of
the smokestack of Hetherington's sawmill in Lockhartville.

Judd O'Brien has been a splitterman since he was
fourteen years old. A splitterman stands in front of the
main circular saw and catches the boards and slabs in his
arms as they fall from the log carriage. The boards he
flips over to the edgerman, who stands a little to his left;
the slabs he propels down the rollers to the slab sawyers.
A splitterman must be strong and tireless and he must
possess an excellent sense of balance since all day long he
sways back and forth within inches of a saw that could
rip him in half almost before he had time to cry out. It's
said there used to be sawmills in Africa where the splitterman sacrificed live cocks to the saw to appease it.

In good years the mill runs from March to October, in
bad years from May to August. The lumber is shipped
overseas; so in bad years the millhands meeting in the
general store or at the filling station say to one another,
"Something's gone wrong in England."

There were horses and oxen in the millyard when I
worked there as a teenager. Now, of course, they've been
replaced by tractors. My father used to draw pictures of
horses which he allowed only the smallest children to see.
Wetting a big rectangular carpenter's pencil with his

tongue, chewing his lower lip, flashing the gold front tooth he'd bought when he was eighteen, he drew fat cart horses with bobbed tails and great round haunches and bellies. He drew such pictures for Stephanie and me, and if I had not seen them then I would never have dreamt that he could have done such a thing. Before I was twelve I had learned to hide my watercolour sketches to avoid his scowl of impatience or sneer of contempt.

From time to time, for one reason or another, he borrowed a horse: perhaps a horse and a two-wheeled dump cart with which to haul home from the mill the board edgings that provided us with free firewood. I helped load and unload the cart, frustrated always by the seeming immensity of the task facing us: the great pyramid of edgings in front of the mill, from which we had to gather up the wood that we stacked in the cart, dumped in our backyard, carried an armful at a time into the woodshed, and stacked again. Armful after armful, cartful after cartful, all day today, all day tomorrow, and all day the day after tomorrow, world without end.

"You're a lazy bugger," my father said, and he was right. I tried frantically to hasten the completion of the task or, failing that, make it appear that we were making rapid headway, a part of my mind trying to trick the rest of it into believing we were almost done when in fact we were only starting. To that end, I'd be scrambling up the pyramid one minute to take my load from the top of it, the next minute running around the base like a tongue licking an ice cream cone. I pried at the edgings with a peavey, not because that made it easier to get at them, but in the hope of starting an avalanche that would create the illusion that the pile had become smaller. I loaded myself down so that I staggered, or I ran with a stick or two in each hand, unable to decide which method was the quickest.

In the meantime, Judd carried his loads, each of them the same size and from almost the same spot. His pace never varied. He neither hurried nor paused to rest. At the end of the day the section of the pyramid where he had been working would appear to have been sliced off by a gigantic knife. And tomorrow he would begin again where he had left off.

It was the same with any job that we did together: peeling pulpwood, cutting hay, thinning carrots.

The eyes of horses magnify men, my father used to say. His father had told him so. He said that to a horse a man appears to be, oh, twelve, maybe fourteen feet tall; if it weren't for that, horses would long since have taken over the world.

The horse and the dog were the only animals in heaven.

To calm his horses, my grandfather, who was a teamster, put his mouth to their ears and whispered. All during my childhood I wondered what he said to them. Eventually I discovered—or did I conjecture?—that he offered them endearments he would never have dared offer a woman. "My darlings, my precious ones, my sweethearts, my pretty ones." I know that's what some of the old men said to their boats.

My father liked riddles. Does a tree make any sound when it falls in an empty wood? When a man's coat has been patched so often that nothing remains of the original cloth is it the same coat or a new one?

"If you ever have to smoke other people's cigarette butts," he once advised me, "if you ever come down to that, if you must pick up butts from the road or street and smoke them, then always be sure you put the burnt end in your mouth. Fire kills germs. That's why you hold a needle in the flame from a match before using it to break a gumboil."

"If you're ever on the bum, tramping," he said another time, and probably more than once, "the best foods to carry with you are bread and cheese, because they last longest and they'll fill you up. But eat an apple whenever you get the chance, for physic, to keep your guts from getting all bunged up."

We are walking side by side, he and I, in a rainbow-coloured tunnel called Saturday Night in Windsor.

45

Saturday Night in Windsor smells of popcorn and fried onions and gasoline and motor oil, and tastes like root beer and hot dogs and licorice cigars.

Saturday Night in Windsor is where Randolph Scott lives, and Rod Cameron, and the Durango Kid, and Red Ryder, and Roy Rogers, and Gene Autrey, and the Human Torch, and Batman, and Frankenstein's Monster.

Saturday Night in Windsor is the King's Own Nova Scotia Highlanders being piped aboard a troop train bound for Halifax, with my brother Patrick among them.

Saturday Night in Windsor is the Highlander who missed the train and stood arguing with the station-master —me wondering how they'd punish him, tasting his anxiety like a surfeit of chocolates.

Saturday Night in Windsor is a newsreel on the sinking of the *Graf Spee*. The guns of the ships are much less powerful than I had imagined. They make such small holes, I complain, such tiny holes—having expected that one shell would be sufficient to cause a ship to disintegrate. How I'd have laughed and clapped my hands then if the pictures had been of Hiroshima!

Now Saturday Night in Windsor is a man with a crooked neck who wants to fist fight with my father, who stands beside me, holding my hand.

"I ain't scared of you, Mosher," my father says. "I'd be damn glad to fight you if I didn't have my little boy with me."

He holds my hand so tight that it hurts. To my astonishment I realize that what he has said is the opposite of the truth. Actually he's glad that I'm here, because he's afraid.

No, that's an oversimplification of my feelings. It's true that I knew what he felt, although I can't have been more than four or five years old at the time; but I didn't give it the name "fear" until years later, during one of my journeys into the past.

Another time: we're lost in the woods, we walk for hours and it's as if we were walking back and forth, and around and around, in a small green room, wondering,

46

Where did the door go? What happened to the windows that used to be here? Everything is watercolour green, except for the sky which is watercolour blue. Seeing that my father is frightened, I giggle, and he calls me a god-damn fool.

Later he tells me about a man he knew who froze to death in the woods. From the man's tracks in the snow the searchers learned that at one point he had wandered out of the forest into one of his own fields, within sight of his own house. That had happened during the afternoon of a clear day, and yet instead of going home the man had turned and gone back into the woods. "You could tell from his footprints that he was runnin'," my father said. "I guess by that time he was so crazy scared he didn't know where he was."

Once a cow has been allowed to run wild in the woods it has to be killed—that was another thing my father used to say. "Somethin' happens to them," he said, "so that they're no good for nothin'; it's somethin' the woods does to them; they have to be killed."

When he was eighteen he went west on a harvest excursion to Saskatchewan, to help harvest wheat, in a colonist car, as they were called, with wooden slats in the berths and no pillows or mattresses unless you could afford to rent them. Out west he drove a team consisting of a horse and a mule; he had a picture of it and claimed all the rest of his life that mules were smarter than horses.

"There was this town in Ontario,"—this was a story he often used to tell—"and just before we got there the conductor came through our car and told us we'd better get down on the floor, because the townspeople might put the rocks to the windows. A while before that a train full of harvesters, they'd stopped there and them fellers they'd ripped that town apart from arsehole to appetite. The townspeople, they was out for revenge."

He has worked for fifty years and never once had a permanent year-round job. He has worked for fifty years and never once had a job that a machine couldn't have done better had there been a machine there to do it.

Every summer he works in the sawmill. In the winter he cuts long lumber if he's lucky and subcontracts to cut pulpwood if he isn't. He prefers the mill, because there he's "sure of his pay," which means he's certain that come payday he'll be handed a cheque and the cheque will be good. "Always try to find a job where you're sure of your pay," he used to say to me, he having learned from bitter experience that this was the most he dared ask of fate: a job where he knew that he was going to be paid.

When you subcontract for pulpwood you may have to walk to the house of the contractor, Tommy Barbour, who is almost as poor as you, and sit in his kitchen for an hour or so, talking about the heat, and the blackflies, and whether or not there'll be a provincial election in the spring, and maybe he'll give you a quart of beer to cut the dust out of your throat (nobody here ever buys beer by the pint). You'll be a little wary of one another, so you'll both work very hard at puttying up the silences. And when finally you start to say what you came for, you'll pretend it's an afterthought, your hand will be on the doorknob. "By the way, Tom old son, while I happen to be here, I was wonderin' if maybe. . . ."

"Ah, Judd boy, I was just goin' to mention it myself! You know how it is, Judd boy. Them jeezly bastards in Hantsport. Won't pay a man a cent before the end of the cut. Not a jeezly cent. Look, boy, I'll give you half of what I got in my pocket. Ten dollars. That's half of every cent I got, Judd boy. And the rest a week from Friday. True as gospel. That's the best I can do, Juddie. You can't get blood out of a turnip, old son."

Always open a package of tobacco from the bottom instead of the top. You waste less that way.

No one ever feared Judd O'Brien except his children. No one ever truly feared him except the youngest of his children, me.

When I was a child I was afraid of mirrors or, rather, of the strange face that stared back at me from the other side of the glass. I would try to trick that face into admitting that it wasn't me. I would blink rapidly, suddenly stick out my tongue, clap my hand to my mouth, but I was never quick enough to achieve my ambition of seeing the person in the mirror betray himself by failing to imitate my gesture in time. "Isn't that funny," the adults said, "Kevin's making faces at himself again."

I was also afraid of high places.

"Me too," somebody said at a party a few nights ago. He had read Freud, of course, and so he added, laughingly, "I suppose we're both of us afraid that we'll jump."

"I used to think so," I said. "Now I suspect I'm more afraid that I'll push somebody off."

"I've never had any murderous instincts," he said nervously. I could see that he, too, was afraid of the looking-glass.

None of this is as tangential as it may seem. We return to the past and change it. What was terrible may become merely distasteful, then ridiculous, then humorous. Or the sequence may be reversed.

The boy Kevin is beaten with a strap. The pain is nothing. What rankles is the rout of the will, the orgastic cession of the last scrap of privacy, the moment of becoming nobody. This is the prototypal sacrament, the boy Isaac lying naked on the altar. . . .

My father is punishing me for murdering him when I was three years old.

Mind you, I need only rephrase it—the naughty boy, Kevin, is being spanked—and it becomes merely distasteful, or ridiculous, or humorous.

There is a painting by Paul Klee of the young Jesus being spanked across his mother's knees. He is naked, and his halo has fallen to the floor.

What would Judd have chosen to be had he been given a choice?

A boxer, I think. Yes, he would have liked to be Jack Dempsey. He has lived all his life among men who settle quarrels with their fists and boots. He's been knocked down a few times when he was drunk, but I doubt that he's ever been in a real fight. I think he'd growl some excuse and sneak away—perhaps not so much from fear as from a

49

kind of wild shyness, for there's nothing he dreads more than being conspicuous.

The last time I saw him there was a picture Scotch-taped to the wall below the clock shelf. It was a centrefold from the *Police Gazette,* showing Dempsey delivering the left hook to the chin that sent Gene Tunney down for the Long Count at Soldier Field in Chicago in 1927.

I have an old snapshot showing a young man with the rectangular body of a heavyweight boxer; he is standing, booted feet apart, on the backs of two harnessed work horses, his arms crossed as if he wanted to put them somewhere out of the way, his smile a little dangerous, as if he were trying very seriously to decide whether the spectators' laughter was for him, or against him. The inscription in ink reads: *Self. Out West. 1923.* He looks a little, a very little, like the young Jack Dempsey.

I'd have included that picture in *The Life and Times of Judd O'Brien.*

The Kodak camera was one of the great communal fetishes of the 1930s, and one of the occult objects of my infancy. Women dressed up as men; men dressed up as women; they clowned with whisky bottles and ukeleles; they simpered and strutted; they enacted little farces and melodramas—all for the camera. Once I unrolled an unprocessed film, impatient to see the pictures, and almost wept in outrage when I found myself entangled in glossy black nothingness.

I have another snapshot, showing a young man and a young woman lying in the grass under a rosebush. The young man looks a little, a very little, like the young Jack Dempsey. His face is proud, but a little sullen. He wears a white shirt, unbuttoned almost to the waist. The young woman is fleshy; there's something nineteenth century and French about her: a Courbet nude except that, of course, she isn't naked, but clothed in a loose flowered dress. She is voluptuous rather than beautiful. Laughing, she shows too many teeth. Her hair tumbles down almost to her breasts.

50

there was
an old
woman
from
wexford

Back in the motel in the early hours of the morning, still
too tense to sleep, Kevin O'Brien (1) eats a lobster roll and
a potato salad from cardboard containers, (2) drinks beer,
(3) glances through the entertainment section of the
Saturday edition of the Montreal *Star*, (4) smokes another
cigarette, and (5) watches the late late show on television
with Michael Landon, the Little Joe Cartwright of *Bonanza*,
playing in *I Was a Teenaged Werewolf*. The best line in
the film is spoken when Michael Landon is identified as the
monster on the grounds that, "It must be him: it's wearing
his jacket!"

Afterwards he makes an unsuccessful attempt to begin a
diary, a journal of his jaunt, as Boswell would have called
it. Almost from the time when he first learned to write he
has made sporadic attempts to keep a diary. The problem
is that he can't resist putting down what he regards at the
moment as important, although he knows very well that
the point of keeping a diary is to record trivia, ideally the
kind of trivia that reconfirms the sympathetic reader as a
member of that great communion, the human race.

He takes a notebook from his briefcase, opens it and
writes in the date. How did the day begin? Interviewing a
federal cabinet minister in Halifax. That was less than
twelve hours ago according to his watch, but in terms of
his present mood it could have happened in the previous
decade. The cabinet minister and the newspaper article in
which Kevin has recorded his remarks represent one
reality, Lockhartville represents another. It is almost as if
he had passed through one of those time warps of science
fiction. The clock and the calendar and the map are such

liars! One day he would write something about that and add it to the contents of the briefcase.

Every child has a past, Kevin reflects, but when we begin to have a personal history, it must mean that our first youth is gone. If I had kept a diary all these years, as I so often resolved to do, by now parts of it would read like notes for an historical novel—and I'm not yet thirty years old!

Yes, and he remembers certain events from as long ago as the previous century, having learned of them by word of mouth before he was old enough to read, or even to know there existed such a thing as History. His grandfather's grandfather, also named Kevin O'Brien, had escaped from the Irish potato famine only to die of cholera on an island off the Nova Scotia coast. But that is not what he remembers; that is what he has learned. What he remembers is that the other Kevin O'Brien, and scores like him, died flopping about on the shores of that island like fish out of water. "That's exactly what they looked like," his grandfather told him. "Like trout dying on the riverbank, God rest their souls." And there is a stone in one of the Lockhartville cemeteries, a ghastly white stone, on which are carved the words: *Kevin Michael O'Brien, 1825-1849*. But no one is buried there. Whatever may be left of the body of Kevin O'Brien, born 1825, died 1849, lies in a mass grave on the island on which he perished. As a child our Kevin O'Brien was a little proud and a little afraid of that stone and that empty grave.

He knows now that he was right to stay in a motel rather than in the old house as on previous visits. The house contained too many ghosts. (As if one ghost weren't more than enough.) Then there were mice and the filthy bedclothes that oppressed his spirit even more than they offended his senses.

He tears up the paper containing his scribblings and drops the scraps in the wastebasket with the food containers, the newspaper and the beer bottle caps. Then he gets into bed, turns off the lights and shuts his eyes. But it is a long time before he falls asleep. He lies there in the darkness, remembering. . . .

52

There was that absolute darkness that is possible only in places where human beings are few and live far apart, a darkness in which the only solids are those close enough to touch. So nothing was substantial except his own body and the bed on which he lay listening to the sound of his grandmother singing.

It was hot. Outside his window the nightjars were whistling. It was strange and a little disquieting to hear birds whistling in the darkness. He had kicked away the quilts and wiggled, more than half asleep, out of his clammy underwear, so that now he lay curled up in the salty smell of his naked body, the moist pubescent odour of himself.

Her singing had awakened him many times during the past month. Sometimes he almost wept; sometimes, although he tried not to admit it to himself, he wished that something, anything, even death, would shut her up, and sometimes he went back to sleep without thinking about it at all.

She had sung "I Come to the Garden Alone." He had heard her sing it often before her illness. "That's a Billy Sunday hymn," she always explained. Proudly. Her brother —one of her brothers, David, who was killed with the Sixth Mounted Rifles, or Joseph, who could drink a forty ouncer of navy rum and shoulder a hogshead of flour without batting an eye—her brother had heard Billy Sunday preach in Boston or Bangor or Portland and afterwards they took up the collection in baskets and every basket was filled to overflowing with five, ten, twenty, fifty and one hundred dollar bills. She described the baskets of money as Mary or Martha might have described the miraculous loaves and fishes.

And she had sung "There Is a Fountain Filled With Blood," while sitting in her rocking chair, a hot brick wrapped in an old sweater or stuffed into an old wool sock pressed hard against her belly to ease the pain, other bricks warming on the back of the wood stove (Enterprise Foundry, Sackville, New Brunswick), the teapot brewing as it always was; she added leaves (Red Rose Orange Pekoe) whenever it became too weak for her taste, emptied them only when there was no room left for water, simply opened the kitchen door and dashed them out into the yard. And what she smelled of was burning wool and ginger cloves and a liniment called Oil of Wintergreen.

There is a fountain filled with blood
Drawn from Emmanuel's veins,
And sinners plunged beneath that flood
Lose all their guilty stains.

The window blinds shrugged like the wings of some enormous mystic bird, like the wings of the blue heron that fed in the swamp between the river and the railroad. He was afraid of the blue heron, had always been afraid of it, yet he would stand sometimes for as long as thirty minutes, spying on it. From the hill overlooking the swamp the bird looked bigger and vastly stronger than he; certainly its legs were longer than his, or so it seemed to him, and he could imagine it running after him—in his imagination it ran rather than flew—and beating him down with its great beak, legs and wings. The wonder that he felt, watching it, was close to worship.

"Mother," a voice said. "Please, Mother." That would be his Aunt Lorna, who would be hugging together the flaps of a faded red wrapper, and who would not have put on her glasses. Her eyes looked naked without glasses —it was the kind of stark white adult nakedness that made him shifty-eyed with embarrassment; and there were faint purplish indentations on her temples. "Keep the Lower Lights A'Burning" his grandmother sang now, her voice louder, much louder, derisive and defiant.

In Aunt Lorna's voice a deep-throated adult sorrow gave way reluctantly to a whine almost like that of a small girl screwing down the lid on a sob. He rolled over in bed and raised his head slightly, listening, but he could not distinguish sentences; only words jutting out like rocks from a river of murmurs. It was as if between the words *mother* and *bed* and *late* and *please*, each of them repeated many times, his aunt were droning wordlessly through her nose with the tip of her tongue pushing hard against her lower teeth.

The old woman wore a black wig shaped like a soup bowl and boasted about her jet-black hair. "There's not many women my age that has hair to compare with mine, with not so much as a wisp of gray in it." She rouged herself with bits of crepe paper moistened with saliva and bragged about the youthful redness of her cheeks. As a young woman, after her husband went to Saskatchewan to harvest wheat and did not return, she had gone into the woods alone, with a horse, an axe and a bucksaw, and come out with wood enough to keep her five small children from freezing although, despite the fire, it got so cold at night that water froze in the kitchen pails.

> She's only a bird in a gilded cage,
> A wonderful sight to see.
> Some think that she's happy and free from
>   care,
> But she's not what she seems to be.

Once, so his grandmother had told him, a cobbler had lived in Lockhartville, a man who made shoes and repaired them. He, Kevin, had never seen a cobbler but could remember visiting a clockmaker with his father. The clockmaker wore either a beard or a great drooping moustache, Kevin could not recall which; his skin was the colour of a plucked chicken, and his hair and suit were the same pepper and salt shade of gray. What he called his shop was only a corner of his living room, a roll top desk and a board covered with purple velvet from which hung a great many pocket watches, some without hands, a few without faces, their inner workings exposed. The house in which he lived, unlike the other houses in the village, was lighted with gas rather than kerosene. Kevin had never seen such white artificial light and the wicks, shaped like the thumbs of mittens but made from transparent gauze, almost mesmerized him. Whenever his grandmother spoke of the cobbler, Kevin gave him the clockmaker's face and hair.

55

The cobbler's name was Tulley Greenough. Just as it seemed important to Kevin that the man had been a cobbler and not, say, a millhand like his father, so it seemed important that his name had been Tulley Greenough and not John Smith or William Jones. Tulley Greenough was a name to savour, like the names of Caleb, the son of Jephunneh the Kenizzite, and Joshua, the son of Nun, who wholly followed the Lord.

One day the cobbler learned there was a cancer in his body, a cancer being an enormous spider that fed on its victim's flesh. (They had taken a tapeworm three yards long from the stomach of her brother Joseph, the old woman said. She had seen it, preserved in a jar of alcohol. And there was the scarlet woman in Wolfville who gave birth to five gray puppies.) Knowing the cancer would eat away his vitals if he did not destroy it, Tulley Greenough cut himself open with a cobbler's knife—cut himself open, snatched out the great hairy black spider and hurled it into the open fire where, clacking and hissing, it died. Its body was as big as a man's two doubled fists.

Kevin got out of bed and groped his way to the window, knelt there with his arms and chin on the ledge, night insects twanging the screen like an out of tune mandolin, a warm breeze that smelled of fresh-cut grass causing his hair to tickle his ears and forehead.

> There goes that Boston burglar,
> In strong chains he'll be bound;
> For some crime or another
> He's being sent to Charlestown.

She had bought an autoharp from a salesman who wore a white linen suit and a straw hat and told her, as she never tired of repeating, that she was a contralto. A contralto. She could interpret dreams and pronounce curses. As a child she had known a witch who made tables dance. She had ridden on a street car in Boston. She could dance a clog, a jig or a hornpipe. She had seen the face of Jesus in the sky. She could make up rhymes. She could live on two dollars a week. And she was a contralto. With jet-black hair and cheeks as apple-red as any sixteen-year-old girl's.

Allister, Kevin's cousin, had despoiled the harp in attempting, with a spike and a pair of pliers, to turn it into a guitar. She entombed the mutilated instrument in a cedar chest, taking it out occasionally before her illness to sing with it cradled, forlorn and silent, in her arms.

> *As I was leaving old Ireland,*
> *All in that month of June,*
> *The birds were singing merrily,*
> *All nature seemed in tune.*

Sing me a song, Granner. I like songs that tell stories best. Tell me a story, Granner. But as he had grown older he had become increasingly ashamed of her. Walking beside her on the street in Windsor. Her with her shopping bag and little frilly pink hat she'd bought at a Pythian Sisters rummage sale. The sight of that hat made him want to die and be buried and lie in his grave for a thousand years before being restored to life. Sometimes he shut his eyes tight and clenched his teeth as though preparing for a merciful bullet through the head.

> *My name is Peter Wheeler,*
> *I'm from a foreign shore.*
> *I left my native country,*
> *Never to see it more.*

And when she insisted on taking him into Livingston's Restaurant for a treat! Maple walnut ice cream with maple syrup sauce. And a root beer. For herself, a pot of tea. The coins knotted up in a handkerchief inside a change purse, the change purse at the very bottom of a handbag, the clasp of the handbag reinforced with a safety pin. Because money was immeasurably valuable, almost sacred She would never accept the copper-coloured five-cent pieces that were being issued because of the war. And she believed that threads of gold were woven into the paper notes—because if they were paper and nothing more what good would they be? When he was much younger she had shown him the threads, holding up a dollar bill to the light. And he had seen them.

Two nickels for the ice cream. One of them bearing a likeness of King George V. Another nickel for the sauce. A dime for the root beer bearing a very faint likeness of King Edward VII. A nickel and one, two, three, four, five pennies for the tea. Each coin the centre of a separate, solemn transaction. And the waitress so reassured by such weakness, so strengthened by it that her eyes shone with power, like Hitler's.

> *Poor Mary she lay at the door*
> *As the wind it blew cross the wild moor.*

But the worst came when she brought out her lunch. A handful of crackers and a scrap of cheese wrapped in greasy brown paper. To be eaten there while the other three billion people in the world looked on and grinned.

Thinking now of the shame he'd felt, Kevin almost blubbered, not so much out of pity for her or guilt at his secret treason, although these were part of it, as from a sudden desolate awareness of how powerless he was, of how little effect his real wishes had on himself, let alone the world that surrounded him.

He went back to bed and covered himself with the quilts. It was still uncomfortably hot but perhaps if he covered himself he would be more likely to fall asleep.

Tell me a story, Granner. "There wasn't a man in the eighteen counties could hold a candle to Joe Casey." That's how one such story began. Joe Casey, her father and Kevin's great-grandfather, had lived in the time when a man produced everything his family used except sugar, tea, rum and tobacco. To obtain the money for sugar and tea (Joe neither smoked nor drank) he sold stove wood in Wolfville and always just before entering the town he reined in his horses, climbed down from his wagon and adjusted his load, propping it up here and there with

58

crooked sticks, so that it would appear to be larger than it was. Joe Casey could fool a townsman into believing a cord was two cords and a half. His daughter was so impressed with his skill that she was still celebrating it more than forty years after his death.

It was in celebration of Joe Casey as much as from poverty or frugality that she carried a stick of chalk to the rummage sales, with which to alter prices—spitting on her fingers and rubbing out one number, using the chalk to substitute another, so that she bought a pair of shoes for fifteen cents rather than a quarter of a dollar. She could as readily have slipped the shoes into her shopping bag and paid nothing. But that would have been theft, and theft was a sin. Thou shalt not steal. But thou shalt be cunning as a serpent. Blessed are they who survive, saith the Lord.

> Tell him since he went away
> How sad has been our lot:
> The landlord came one winter's day
> And turned us from our cot.

And another candle was lit to the memory of Joe Casey when she scavenged at the Windsor dump, gathering pumpkins that had grown there and selling them from door to door. Grown right in the country, Missus, the way the good Lord intended, with no fertilizer except manure. Nothin' like that hothouse stuff they sell in the stores. Fresh country-grown pumpkins. Thou shalt not lie for thou art a Baptist who was put under the water in December after a hole had been chopped in the river ice. But thou shalt outwit the townsmen for thereby cometh glory, and it is good in mine eyes. And thou shalt strive always to survive.

"Mother," this time it was the voice of Kevin's father and Kevin could see him as clearly as with his eyes. Shoe-less, gray wool socks darned with yarn of another colour, Levis pulled on over long-sleeved flannel underwear, the underwear partially unbuttoned because of the heat, thick curly gray hair on his chest, a belt, and suspenders that bore the word "Police" on their clasps as though designed

for small boys playing cops and robbers. Saying, "You
can't sit here like this all night, Mother," although he knew
well enough that she could, and would.

> Oh, saddle up my blackest horse
> My gray is not so speedy,
> And I'll ride all night and I'll ride all day
> Till I overtake my lady.
>
> Tum-a-link-tum-tum-me-ah-lie,
> Tum-a-link-tum-ty-tee,
> I'll ride all night and I'll ride all day
> Till I overtake my lady.

"Mother, Mother, Mother," said Judd O'Brien, who
had said the same thing in almost exactly the same tone a
year earlier when he discovered that, by swearing that her
adult children were unable to support her, she had per-
suaded the parish overseer of the poor to pay her two
dollars a week.

The two dollars came with Perry Sandford the mailman
who drove a Ford except when there was so much snow
or mud that he had to harness his roan mare to a buggy
or sleigh; and on the day it arrived the old woman enacted
several rituals to render herself invisible, putting on a coat
and hat she did not wear at any other time—a short black
cloth coat with a collar, cuffs and hem of artificial fur, and
a sky-blue cloche (she could dance the fox-trot and
Charleston and never dreamed there were changing
fashions in either clothes or dances). She went out the
front door that was otherwise used only by radio licence
inspectors, Jehovah's Witnesses, Mormons, peddlers and
strangers asking the way to Truro or Halifax. She walked
down the road, no matter how deep the snow was, or the
mud, head down, limping a little, and met Perry out of
sight of her son's house. He drove her to a store in a
neighbouring village where she cashed the cheque and
bought a little treat, a bag of peppermints or maple buds,
a loaf of raisin bread that for some unknown reason she
always called plum loaf, a bottle of ginger beer, a half-
dozen hot cross buns or a jelly roll. (And, oh God, what a

sacramental interchange it was, the offering and acceptance of a tumbler half-full of soft drink, a small slice of pastry spread with jellied strawberries. Kevin quailed at the memory of it like one who is suddenly aware that he has been paid an honour he neither earned nor desired yet is too cowardly to refuse.) What was left of the money went into the cedar chest. "I've got the money to bury me," she boasted defiantly.

Oh western wind when wilt thou blow
That the small rain down may rain?
Christ that my love were in my arms
And I in my bed again.

And before he died there was such a hole in Joe Casey's throat that the tea he drank ran out through it and down his collar. He went to the barn and back on all fours and his last words, spoken to his wife who had offered to fetch him water, were: "Nobody has to wait on Joe Casey. Joe Casey can look after himself."

Now Kevin's father and aunt were talking together on the stairs. "That look in her eyes, Judd, when I talked to her; I don't think she even knew who I was, I swear I don't; she'll be dead by mornin' if she keeps this up, you mark my words, she'll be dead by mornin'."

"There's nothin' on God's green earth we can do for her, Lorna, you know that as well as I do, you heard what the doctor said."

"But he could give her somethin' maybe, somethin' to make her sleep."

"I'll be damned if he could, not if she didn't want him to. I don't know how she's hung on as long as she has, so help me God, I don't."

"Well, there's somethin' to be thankful for, the kids are asleep."

There was a wild colonial boy,
Jack Dugan was his name.
He was born and bred in Ireland,
At a place called Castlemaine.

61

Kevin did not know how long he had been awake. Perhaps he had slept and reawakened. He had heard her sing many songs, that was certain. But perhaps there had been times when he had only dreamt that he heard her singing. He was almost as unsure of the duration and sequence of events as he had been years before when he was delirious with pneumonia.

Should he go to the kitchen and talk with her? He had considered doing so, but was held back by fear; he was always afraid of the sick and unlike many of his fears this one was not coupled with an irresistible fascination. He was terrified of high places, yet climbed the tallest trees and cliffs, almost choking with the exaltation of it. But the fear inspired by the sick only made him shrink back into himself like a rabbit.

He found himself sitting on the couch in the kitchen. He was wearing his brown suit, a white shirt and a necktie, but his feet were bare. As always, the wool pants made his legs itch, and he wondered why he had put them on, together with the jacket, especially when it was so hot.

A gas lamp hung from the ceiling, replacing the kerosene lamp that normally stood on the table by the window. His grandmother sat where she always sat, with her autoharp in her arms, but all its strings had been restored.

And there was a third person in the room.

He was a man whose picture Kevin had seen in a book.

It was a very old book and had long since disappeared. His mother had read to him from it before he could read. He remembered a poem with the refrain *curfew shall not ring tonight* and another that contained the lines:

> *Morgan, Morgan the raider,*
> *And Morgan's terrible men,*
> *With Bowie knives and pistols*
> *Come galloping down the glen.*

Those poems were among the visions he had experienced in the dream time of infancy. They were one with the orchid he had brought home from a forbidden visit to the swamp and the falling star he had seen explode like a

Roman candle when, in broad daylight, it crashed into the backyard.

There were pictures with the poems. In fact the pictures were part of the poems. There was a girl in a long white dress, swinging from the tongue of a bell that hung in a tower so tall that the top of it must have pricked the sky. There was a boy who wore a sword and spurs, one hand grasping his horse's saddle, the other reaching out to a woman; she, too, wore a long white dress.

And there was a picture that, as far as he could recall, did not connect with anything else.

A man sat at a desk surrounded by books and manuscripts and test tubes. He wore a costume that Kevin had later seen again in pictures of Keats, Byron and Shelley. And he was staring at a skull. It was the skull that had fascinated Kevin. Often, while looking at it, he had pressed his fingers against his face so as to feel his own skull under its thin jacket of flesh. He had never looked so closely at the man, yet the picture might not have excited him so much if the man had not been there. And now the man was sitting not eight feet away from him.

Neither the man nor the old woman seemed to be aware of Kevin's presence. She was performing for this man, Kevin realized, as she had performed for that other man in the white suit and the straw hat.

> As I was going to Derby town
>   All on a market day,
> I met the biggest ram, sir,
>   That ever fed on hay.
>
> And didn't he ramble!
>   He rambled up and down,
> And all around the town,
>   He rambled till the butcher cut him down.

She laughed and, awakening again in his own bed, Kevin heard her laughing. Her laughter was so joyous that it tickled the nerves in Kevin's throat so that he also laughed.

63

Now this ram he had two horns, sir,
  Two horns made out of brass,
And one came out of his head, sir,
  The other came out of his arse.

And didn't he ramble!
  He rambled up and down,
And all around the town,
  He rambled till the butcher cut him down.

"And what do you say to that, you old bugger? Tell me straight out now, you old fart, what do you say to that?"

"Mother, please," Lorna said.

"Mother, for God's sake," said Judd.

"Here's another for you, you old shitarse," said Kevin's grandmother, and she sang:

There was an old woman from Wexford,
  In Wexford she did dwell,
Who loved her husband dearly,
  But another man twice as well!

Next morning when Kevin got up she was lying down in her room upstairs but by then it no longer mattered; the doctor had been there and gone and that didn't matter either. But it mattered very much, not only then but ever afterwards, that his grandmother, an old peasant woman, had sat up all through the last night of her life, singing songs to entertain herself and Death.

kevin
and
stephanie

Is my sister Stephanie dead, like my grandmother, my
mother and my brother?

I can't remember.

It isn't normal to forget such a thing. I must be going
crazy.

That is part of a dialogue that Kevin conducts with himself in his motel room before he is fully awake.

Of course as soon as he regains consciousness he knows
that Stephanie is alive, or rather that he has no reason to
suppose that she might be dead.

It has been several years since he heard from her, but
only last night Judd told him that she was now living in
Montreal. "She's changed her name so often that sometimes I can't write to her because I don't remember what
name to put on the envelope," Judd said.

"Poor Stevie," Kevin said. There had been no dramatic
rupture in the relationship between him and his sister;
they had grown up, and life had carried them in different
directions, that was all.

"I bet if you seen her now you wouldn't know who she
was," Judd said.

"She used to be beautiful," Kevin said.

Judd looked uncomfortable. He was suspicious of words
such as "beautiful." "She was here to see me one day last
summer," he said, slowly.

"And she'd changed a lot?" Kevin prodded him.

"She had this goddamn purple grease on her eyes,"
Judd said.

Kevin laughed.

"Made her look like a goddamn corpse," Judd said. His
face showed he did not like Kevin's laughter. "And there

was this goddamn fool with her," he said; the liquor had loosened his tongue. "He had hair down over his ears, and he was wearin' them Christless sandals. Like a woman. And he must of been fifty years old if he was a day."

"Have another drink," Kevin said.

It was apparent that Judd was seeing Stevie's companion in his mind's eye, and hating what he saw. "The son of a bitch was drivin' a car about a million miles long," he said. There was a silence while Judd drank. Then, "They kept callin' each other 'darling'," he said. And he repeated the word, spitting it out as if it were a nauseating object that he had put in his mouth by mistake: "Darling!"

"Poor Stevie," Kevin repeated.

"I pity her kids more'n I pity her," Judd said. The two children of Stephanie's marriage were being reared by their paternal grandparents. "Christ, there's no reason why anybody should pity Stevie. She's livin' high off the hog and havin' the time of her life."

"Do you really believe that?" Kevin asked.

Judd stared at him. "Well, she looks a helluva lot more prosperous than you do, boy," he said with a half-contemptuous laugh. It was too late now for him to break his old habit of despising his son. Then, as if in placation, Judd began to reminisce about the years when Kevin and Stephanie were children. "It seems like it was only yester-day," he said.

"Everything seems like it was only yesterday," Kevin said. But of course almost nothing that Judd remembered about the children Kevin and Stephanie had ever actually happened, for he had never really known either of them. As he talked, made garrulous by alcohol, Kevin's mind wandered.

And now Stephanie was—what? A belly dancer? Perhaps. A stripper? Possibly. Mistress to a politician? Very likely it was something like that. A call girl? That was even more probable. Her only capital was her body.

He hears voices outside his motel room and the sound of cars being started. The cars do not start easily; it must be a cold morning. He leans back with his hands under his head and his elbows extended, letting his mind go back to a time when there existed an entity known as Kevin-and-Stephanie.

The sky is October orange and from the heath the upstairs windows on the west side of the house are the colour of brass.

Kevin and Stephanie have come from the farm of their friends, the Lindsays, where they ran like mice along beams thirty feet above the floor, pulled themselves through windows three storeys high out on to a sloping roof and leapt, with roller-coaster screams, into a trampoline of hay.

There is chaff in their nostrils and sweat has mucilaged chaff to their bodies. Perhaps they've seen a red fox running or startled a grazing deer that first froze, sniffing the wind, and then bolted, its white tail bobbing.

Kevin and Stephanie. Kev and Stevie. They've heard their names coupled so often and for so long that now it seems the coupling not only represents but helps create something that incorporates both of their public selves. At the same time, by its sheer formality, it causes their private selves to shrink back, so that this Kevin-and-Stephanie is simultaneously a little more and immeasurably less than Kevin or Stephanie alone.

They are brother and sister. They've been told that brothers and sisters love one another, and they believe it.

He has also been told that he is pale and thin. He wants to die young like Keats, and in one of his dreams he is a ghost fingering his parents' sorrow. His mouth is hungry and faintly girlish, or even womanly; he squints because he has learned that his blue-gray eyes make the adults uneasy.

She is taller and tanned the colour of a gingersnap, with many small faint scars and bruises on her arms and legs. Her eyes, in which the blue predominates, are either wide with an almost animal innocence or dully and hopelessly

furtive. When they play hide and seek among the outbuild-
ings, she shuts every door behind her, including those
that are almost always open, and is one of the first to be
found. He scrambles into a tree, sits there (where they
have only to look up to see him), and watches them
crouch and crawl and peer into all the dark and secretive
places. Once or twice he has almost convinced himself
that he can make himself invisible, like one of his favourite
radio heroes, The Shadow.

He says something to her now. "It's time I went for the
cows." The cows belong to a neighbour and sometimes
when Kevin fetches them from the high pasture two miles
away he pretends that he is a Swiss goat boy and that the
hills are the Alps. There are thirty cows and he has given
each of them a name. But that doesn't matter now, because
whatever he says is only an excuse to get away.

"You don't have to ask my permission," she answers
tauntingly.

He leaves her standing by the barbed wire fence with
elderberry, touch-me-not and golden rod around her.

It's cool and the cedars tremble a little in the wind.
There is an interval in which nothing happens.

She tears off a blade of grass and puts it in her mouth,
but it is so bitter and juiceless that she immediately spits
it out.

Her fingernails pry off a scab from her forearm. She digs
a little hole in the earth with the toe of her sneaker.

Then she sees something running—or flying—toward
her.

A bear or an ape with wings.

A bat half as big as a man.

An old man with arms outstretched under his cloak so
that it seems that he possesses wings.

An old man in a black mask. An old man with a staff.
An old man almost flying.

"Heh! Heh! Heh!"

Stephanie runs.

The barbed wire tears her cotton dress, scrapes her skin
so the blood runs down her arms and thighs. She falls to

her knees on stones, the pain a vertigo of humiliation. She bounds over tree stumps and boulders.

And he runs after her.

Or flies.

"Heh! Heh! Heh!"

She snatches off her shoes, and carrying them in her hands, splashes through swampy places where the water is almost up to her knees and the black mud forms blobs between her toes.

She rolls down slopes and clambers up them on all fours. Spruce, pine and fir seem to reach out to grab her; alders and birches whip the bare arms with which she tries to protect her face.

She runs farther and farther from the house, deeper into the woods, like the stepdaughter in a fairy tale.

She keeps on running even after her pursuer screams, "Heh! Heh! Heh!" for the last time, and disappears.

Perhaps it is not really so violent as that. Perhaps the barbed wire is blackberry bush and the stones are gravel; perhaps she is beaten by the mullein rather than by the birches.

Perhaps she is laughing as she runs. The driver of a passing car catching a glimpse of them might think what a pretty picture it made, the two children, one in an outlandish costume, sprinting across the heath and into the trees.

"The country," such a driver might say to his companion, "it's still the best place to bring kids up."

When Stephanie comes back from the woods and lies in the tall grass near the henhouse, her chest heaving like an injured bird, Kevin reappears and asks what's happened to her, and she answers, "Nothing. I was running, that's all."

He is able to believe, almost, that she does not know the identity of her pursuer. And perhaps she too is almost able to believe that she does not know.

She would never run from her brother Kevin, because she is bigger, stronger and faster than he.

Another time there was a fire.

The sawmill whistle has blown three times and the yard of the O'Brien house is full of cars, some with their lights on. Men have come from the airport wearing mechanics' coveralls, and from the sawmill bunkhouse in Levis and checked shirts, and from nearby farms in rubber boots and pale gray overalls. There are even a few student pilots, incongruous because they look so dressed up in their tunics and neckties. The mechanics and airmen move very cleanly and purposefully, as though they were playing baseball. The millhands appear clumsy in comparison, taking shorter and quicker steps as they run between the well and the house, but they spill less water. The farmers, older men, prefer to stand at the well filling buckets, or on the roof emptying buckets as they're handed up to them. The airport men laugh a good deal and because of their laughter the millhands curse and bellow as though the fire were worse than it is; they also call Judd and Leah O'Brien by their first names as often as possible to show that they are friends, that they belong here, that it isn't a goddamn joke to them, the O'Briens getting burnt out. The farmers, most of them, are silent.

Kevin and Stephanie stand in the open doorway of the wagonshed. They feel unnaturally, almost feverishly alert, as children do sometimes when they're snatched suddenly from sleep. They wear only their underpants and the blankets their mother threw around them after she pulled them out of their beds. Their bare feet are cold, so they tread the floor like restless horses. "It's fun to watch grown men run," Stephanie says, and Kevin knows what she means. The men, many of them, are so earthbound that they seem to run slower than they could walk, the water spilling out of their buckets and over their legs and feet.

They talk about how terrible the fire is, repeating things they've heard the adults say. Kevin says, "Fire is a good friend, but a bad enemy," a pronouncement he has heard his father make uncounted times. He envies the men on the bucket brigade. Earlier, when the fire was at its height, there was talk of chopping a hole in the roof; and men were yelling to one another about going back to the bunkhouse for an axe, although most of them must have known that Judd O'Brien possessed not one axe but several and when he was drunk boasted that he was the best god-damn axeman in the eighteen counties of Nova Scotia. Kevin had always loved watching his father on the roof when he climbed there to shingle or whitewash or repair the chimney. It was one place where he, Kevin, had never gone. When he was much younger he imagined that his father was the only man in the world who walked about on rooftops.

"Looks as if we've got her by the balls now," one of the millhands says.

"Yeah, looks like we've cornered the Jesus bitch," another answers.

It intrigues Kevin that the men speak of the fire as if it were an animal, or even a human. It's as though they believed they were doing battle with a dragon.

"It's terrible, all of it," the children keep repeating to each other. They say things like:

"Maybe we'll have to move in with Aunt Lorna."

"She'd never take us. We'd have to go to an orphanage."

But secretly they're thrilled by the fire as though by a visit from an unknown uncle bearing unexpected gifts.

They're a little drunk with the strangeness of it, the dislocation.

"You know something, Lebuba?" Stephanie asks. It's a name she calls him sometimes when they're alone together, a name she first called him in the ancient time when it was as close as she could come to pronouncing "Little Brother."

"You know something, Lebuba? I could hit you if I wanted to and nobody would care."

He looks at her in astonishment, stirs uneasily in his blankets. "What you want to hit me for?"

"Just for fun," she answers. "Just for fun and because nobody would care."

"You hit me and I'll kill you."

"They'd hang you if you killed me," she says patiently. "And besides, you couldn't even if you wanted to. You aren't big enough. Not by a long shot."

71

At first she sounded almost casual. Now she is dancing with excitement. He can see, in the light from the cars, that she is grinning.

"Go to hell," he says to her, helplessly.

She punches him in the belly with both her fists and when he strikes out at her she pinions his arms, easily, and knees him in the groin.

He yelps, then bursts into tears. She steps back a little and slaps his face.

"I'll tell," he says, hating himself for resorting to so infantile a threat. "I'll tell. You see if I don't."

"Tell all you want," she says. "Nobody will care."

He cries so loudly that their mother comes to ask them what's wrong. And Stephanie in her I-am-such-a-grown-up-young-lady voice says, "He's scared, that all; he's scared the house is going to burn down, and we'll be put in an orphanage."

"You're too big for that, Kevin. I've got enough troubles without you acting like a baby. Straighten up or you'll get something to cry about."

She goes back toward the house. "See?" Stephanie says. "Didn't I tell you?" And he stands there in silence, wishing both his mother and sister had died in the fire.

Kevin and Stephanie. Kev and Stevie. They'll walk down the dirt road to the United Church Sunday School, slightly subdued, both of them, by their costumes; her silky pink frock and crinoline and pink sailor hat that from the front seems to hang suspended like a pink moon behind, rather than on, her head; his starched white shirt, flannel shorts and Royal Stewart clip-on bow-tie.

One of them sits naked on a kitchen chair, reading Blue Beetle or Captain Marvel and waiting to step into the washtub in front of the stove as soon as the other, now sitting naked in the water, leaves it.

One waits, silent but with every muscle and membrane from belly to forehead tensed for the plunge into weeping, while the other, already howling, lies, pants down around the ankles, across Judd O'Brien's knees. Judd O'Brien's hand, with nails the like of which Kevin has seen only on other men's feet, makes sounds that in everything except volume resemble rifle cracks.

Years pass. The entity Kevin-Stephanie has almost ceased to exist. Time and space, dream and reality are rocks now rather than clouds. Everything is more distinct and separate than before. Stephanie drives to Halifax with young men her father calls spivs—pool-hustling, harmonica-playing, light-fingered young men, many of them with soft brown eyes, who almost absent-mindedly steal worthless or nearly worthless things which they immediately afterwards throw away or break. Kevin sings "The Blue Skirt Waltz" and "Dance, Ballerina, Dance" and imagines that he is in love with a girl called Natalie.

It is on a Sunday (days have names now) and Kevin is lying on the heath, firing his .22 calibre rifle at a yellow Sportsman's cigarette package that he's hung from a cedar bough. He has bought long rifle cartridges—although for target shooting he doesn't need them—because they look deadlier and he likes the name *Long Rifle*. It reminds him of Hawkeye, The Long Carbine. The rifle sights are so bad that he has to aim very low and far to the left—in fact he must aim at an imaginary target in order to hit the real one. He rather likes that too.

"Hi, Lebuba," Stephanie says.

She is standing above him, barefoot, in red pedal pushers, her yellow blouse partly unbuttoned and knotted above her navel, and she is eating a peach.

"How come?" he asks.

"You sound like an Indian," she says. "How come what?"

"How come you're back already?"

"Did you ever hear the story about the Chinese laundryman named No Come who married a woman named No Come Too? When they had a baby they named it How Come You Come."

He fires at the letter "O" in the word "Sportsman" that is written in invisible ink on a three and one-half by four-inch patch of sky.

"Dead-eye Dick," Stephanie says.

"Yeah," he answers.

"You're not very talkative today, Lebuba."

"I'm thinking," he says, firing again.

"Want a bite?" she offers him the peach.

"No," he growls. Then, with the faintest hint of apology, "No, thanks."

"It's a hell of a life, Lebuba. You know that?"

For the first time he notices that she has been crying. "You look like a little girl," he says. "A little girl about ten years old. Those red eyes, and that peach."

"You think too damned much, Lebuba."

He has knocked the cigarette package off the bough. She nudges his ribs with her toes. "Stop that, for God's sake," he says. He sits up and swings around, facing her.

She dances away. "I've got a target for you, Lebuba." She holds up the partly eaten peach. "Look! You can shoot this out of my hand! Like William Tell! I'll even put it on my head. Yes. That's it. I'll put it on my head." She balances the fruit on her head and stands laughing, her hands on her hips, about twenty feet away. "Come on, Lebuba! Shoot."

He shivers, although the day is warm. "Stevie," he says, "for God's sake."

The peach falls from her head. She catches it and puts it back. "Come on, Lebuba! You can do it!"

He rubs his moist left palm on his jeans. His right hand still holds the rifle. "Go to hell," he tells her.

"Kevin is a scaredy cat!" She comes about five feet closer. "There, you can't miss now. Shoot, you little scaredy cat!"

"Don't be a baby, Stevie," he says. "Don't be such a Jesus goddamn son of a bitch baby."

She comes so close he could touch her with the rifle.

"There, you can't miss now, Lebuba. So shoot."

He lifts the rifle, hesitates for an instant, and then throws

74

it as far as he can. There is the sound of splintering wood as the stock strikes a boulder.

She laughs, not in surprise but mockingly. He turns away and walks toward the house. His whole body is shaking and it is very difficult for him to focus his eyes. The sky is October orange and the upstairs windows on the west side of the house are the colour of brass.

the
kneeling
of the
cattle

Once again Kevin drives from the motel to Lockhartville,
this time in the morning, having first breakfasted on toast
and coffee and stopped at a Nova Scotia Liquor Control
Board store for a forty-ounce bottle of rum and a case of
twenty-four pints of beer. It is a crisp, cool, sunlit day, and
the fields and trees are thinly coated with frost and snow.
He wonders if he should seek out Annie Laurie MacTavish,
she of the improbable name, whose eyes were brown and
green and gold, the colours of a pheasant, and whose
breasts were like live birds in his hands—like live birds
that fly into the house and exhaust themselves trying to
get out. When you take them in your hands you feel the
life pulsating within, and it is like the mild shock of static
electricity.

   He touched Annie Laurie MacTavish's breasts only once
and briefly; yet he remembers the moment as one of the
happiest in his life. In comparison, the later time when he
first entered the body of a woman (a woman named Laura
Trenholm) is only as memorable as the first time that he
got truly drunk. He and Laura spent many nights together,
lying naked in each other's arms; he once knew her body
as thoroughly as he knows the geography of Lockhartville.
There was not a square inch of her that he did not see,
touch and taste. Yet the memory of the pleasure he derived
from her is not nearly so sweet as the memory of Annie
Laurie MacTavish sitting on his lap when they were
passengers together in a half-ton truck that carried Lockhartville adolescents to and from Windsor on Saturday
nights.

   There was a roof and walls on the back of the truck, and
as many as twenty boys and girls were crowded into it,

the warmth of their bodies providing more than sufficient heat even in the dead of winter. Annie Laurie MacTavish wore ski pants and a heavy jacket, and he wore a windbreaker and gloves, so their flesh never touched. The truck rocked and swayed and lurched so that he had to hold her tightly to keep her from falling off his knees. Her hair tickled his face. She smelled of cologne. And sometimes the heat and the movement of the truck lulled her to sleep, and he had to tighten his grip; at such times he was not only willing but eager to give his life for her.

The twenty or so of them would sing silly songs as they rumbled through the winter's night in their overgrown sardine can:

> Sally's gone, yes, Sally's gone;
> She tried to light the fire at early dawn.
> To light the fire more quickly
> She poured in gasoline—
> And now the kitchen's empty, Sally's gone.

"Whatever happened to Annie Laurie MacTavish?" he asks Judd, after they've had their first drink.

"Rod MacTavish's girl? She's a nun. She went into a convent. She's in Africa or India or South America or somewhere. All the MacTavishes are religious. Old Bernard MacTavish, her grandfather, religion drove him crazy."

Kevin laughs at himself. Holy St. Simeon the Mad, he prays, may Sister Annie Laurie MacTavish have only gentle memories of me.

He and Judd devote the day to getting quietly drunk together, and he begins to think that perhaps things used to be better than he is inclined to remember them.

For instance, there was Christmas, as described in another of the manuscripts in his briefcase. For today at least he is prepared to believe that what he said then was true.

At midnight on Christmas Eve, so my grandmother told me when I was a small boy, the cattle kneel in their stalls in adoration of the Christ Child, who was born in a stable.

When I got to be about eight years old I asked her if she had ever seen them kneel. "Of course not," she said. It was not a sight that God permitted human beings to see. She had heard of a man who hid in his barn, hoping to spy on the cattle. In punishment, God struck him blind.

She lived in Nova Scotia, but she might as easily have been an old peasant woman in Galicia or Moldavia.

Years later I learned from a poem by Thomas Hardy that the legend of the kneeling cattle flourished among the peasantry of the old pre-industrial England. For all I know, it may have originated in the Middle Ages, or earlier.

The North Atlantic wind hurled itself against the house, roaring like a demented bear. The snow was piled in great Himalayan drifts between barn and house, so that there was a howling white valley between. Beyond the whiteness of the snow and the blackness of the night, the cattle sank to their knees in a barn warmed by the heat of their own bodies. There, to borrow a phrase from Robert Graves, is the iconotrophic instant, the sacred picture, that best represents the Christmas of my earliest childhood.

We were poor. So poor that my memories of that poverty sometimes seem to me to be less private recollections than dark glimpses of the collective unconscious, dreams from another country and another century.

In 1932, the year I was born, my father worked in the lumber woods for thirty dollars a month. Thirty dollars a month! That sounds absurd, almost comical now—like something out of an Al Capp comic strip or *The Beverly Hillbillies* about the going wage in Pineapple Junction or Bugtussle.

It wasn't funny then.

We were poor. And this was a poverty unlike that which afflicted the urban middle class during the Depression. That kind of poverty compared with ours as a hit-and-run accident, in which the victim escapes death or serious injury, compares with a congenital and incurable disease.

Yet I don't recall a year when there wasn't a Christmas.

The year without a Christmas! That has been the subject of innumerable reminiscences. The child wakes up Christmas morning to find the expected miracle hasn't taken place; and his parents can only murmur lame excuses, laugh nervously and refuse to meet his eyes.

That never happened to me.

It has been said that hunger is the best spice. And it has been said that the good thing about hitting yourself on the head with a hammer is that it feels nice when you stop. About the only good thing about involuntary poverty is that, sometimes, it turns lead into gold.

If the three wise men had been wiser they'd have known they needn't bring gold, frankincense and myrrh to the Christ Child. He'd have been equally happy with a shiny button, a little sugared milk and a single flower.

I can't recall that any new decorations were ever bought for our tree. There were two strands of crepe paper rope, one red and one green, a box of hollow coloured glass balls, a tinsel star for the top, and some odds and ends of things. Every Christmas the ropes were a bit shorter, and there were one or two fewer glass balls. But there always seemed to be enough.

If new decorations had appeared I think we children would have been vastly pleased—but only at first; then we'd have begun to worry. It would have been a superstitious kind of worry. I think we'd have knocked on wood or performed some similar rite of exorcism if we'd been confronted with a third strand of paper rope or another box of glass balls. For the old decorations weren't simply pretty things we hung on a tree; they were Christmas. We were even a little uncomfortable, just for an instant, if we happened to see them at any other time of year. To a small child they looked so dead, thrown together in a heap in their cardboard box in a closet.

There were foods we ate only at Christmas, never at any other time. In retrospect I suppose it was poverty that caused us to eat grapes, oranges and nuts only at Christ-

mas. But we didn't think of it that way at the time; we
no more expected grapes in July than we expected snow.
Those delicacies were sacramental to the season. At least
that's what we children felt. It was as though Christ had
ordained that they should be eaten in honour of his birth.

Consider the grapes. They were always red grapes,
incidentally, never purple or green. The texture of those
grapes was like a kiss. And they offered a trinity of tastes
—the hot roughness of the skin, the cool secret inner pulp,
so full of juice that you both drank and ate of it, and the
crisp nutty seeds you broke between your teeth. Occasionally, when we were almost satiated, we separated skin,
pulp and seeds and ate them one after the other, so that the
flavour of each was distinct. It was a religious rite, the
eating of those grapes, although we didn't need to call it
religious.

Oranges. We ate peel and seeds as well as pulp, and it
was like swallowing a piece of summer that had been rolled
into a ball and preserved in honey. The pulp was as sweet
as sunlight, the skin as acidulous as sunburn.

And nuts. The strange, almost sinister crab-shaped
hearts of the walnuts, the meaty, slightly woody texture
and taste of them. The white meat of the Brazil nuts that
tasted like cake frosting. The rubbery bittersweet hazel
nuts. The protracted spiciness of the almonds. The peanuts,
so salty and oily that they tasted almost fishy. We opened
them with a claw hammer or a piece of stove wood, never
having heard of nutcrackers.

There was ribbon candy, a corkscrew-shaped rainbow
of colours and flavours: mint, banana, wintergreen, lemon,
orange, cherry, and strawberry. Cinnamon sticks: tiny
cherry-pink walking sticks, the cinnamon encased in
molasses candy. And barley toys, which we always ate last
because they were shaped like little animals, tigers, horses
and camels, which we hesitated to destroy—and, besides,
they tasted like nothing except sugary water.

Dinner was chicken and roast pork. But after eating
fruit, nuts and candy all morning, we children were never
very excited about dinner.

81

The gifts were mostly home-made, except for the occasional doll or box of crayons. Once there was a team of wooden horses, hand-carved with a jack-knife and complete with harness and waggon. Another time, a miniature ship, a tern schooner, made with the same jack-knife, and with every sail in working order. Still another time, a home-made bow and arrows, accurate and powerful enough to kill a rabbit or a partridge, although I never used them for that. And if there was no new doll, there was a hand-made wardrobe for the old one.

But the gifts were never so important as the feasting.

All the great holy days down through history have been feasts. That was true in ancient Greece and Rome. It was true in the Middle Ages and during the Renaissance. It is true to a certain extent even today. In fact I suspect that the very conception of the holiday originated in prehistoric times when the hunters came home with meat and the people prepared a great feast, a festival.

The adults in that grim time and place must have felt about their chicken and pork much as we children felt about our fruit, nuts and candy. They were men and women who from childhood had known the sour taste of hunger.

Christmas afternoon, the men drank. The women, at least in my memory, seem to have spent most of the day looking after babies; many of them had several. And they talked, with diaper pins in their mouths, of matters the children weren't supposed to know about. But the men drank. And everything they drank was home-made. Malt beer, molasses beer, spruce beer, hard cider and moonshine.

They did their drinking in the barn. "Come out and take a look at the new cow and tell me what you think of her." That, or something very much like it, meant: Come and have a drink. Or, if there was no barn, and no cow, there was a woodshed. Then it was, "Come and see if you think the bucksaw needs filing." They weren't fooling the women but, then, they weren't really trying to fool them.

Often there was music. Sometimes the only instrument was a fiddle. Sometimes there was an improvised orchestra whose members, if they chose, came or went in the middle of a tune. There might be a violin, a mandolin, a guitar, a banjo, a mouth organ, an autoharp. Somebody might play the spoons or the comb and tissue, both of which are precisely what their names suggest. And there would be step-dancing. The first black man I ever knew was a farmhand who vied with my grandmother for the distinction of being the best step-dancer in the parish. Some of their most spirited competitions took place in our kitchen at Christmas, the two of them facing one another less as dancers than as choreographers. The trick was to improvise new and increasingly complicated movements involving, towards the end, almost every part of the body.

When I come to think about it, it was all very religious. Religious in the subconscious and mystical rather than in the liturgical and public sense. It was the human spirit finding joy in an almost intolerable environment. Even the gods must sometimes envy man's gift of laughter.

the
coming
of age

"I won't stay away so long next time," Kevin says. "Maybe
I'll come home for Christmas."

Home! Perhaps Kevin's is the last generation to be so
enveloped in the atmosphere of one house and one neigh-
bourhood that, however remote, it always remains *home*.

Judd eyes him dubiously. "Yeah, that would be great,"
he says.

A little later Judd falls asleep as abruptly as a child. He
lies on his couch, snoring. From time to time his body is
jerked almost upright by the force of an explosive nasal
honk. The stove crackles, and effuses the fragrance of
burning wood. Kevin puts on his coat and goes upstairs,
where it seems colder than outdoors: the kitchen is the
only room that is heated. The house has deteriorated so
badly that several of the stair steps threaten to give way
beneath him. From the second floor windows the remnants
of lace curtains dangle like the shreds of timeworn battle
flags. Even when he was a child the second floor was only
physically and never psychologically a part of the house.
It was a place where things were stored and forgotten,
a place where children played; occasionally someone slept
here, but no one ever really *lived* here. Life went on
downstairs, chiefly in the kitchen. The second floor was
Baffin Land.

He enters a room that contains a chair, a three-legged
table, a roll top desk and a trunk; a naked bedspring leans
against a wall. When it was not unbearably cold the teenaged Kevin often came here to read or write or moon. Poor
little fool, he saved every issue of *Time* and *Reader's
Digest*, so that this room held stacks of them, which he
perused again and again, thinking to learn more about

the world. Looking around him now he sees that the magazines are gone, but that a few books remain, scattered about the floor. He picks up a number of them and glances at their titles: *Joe's Luck*, by Horatio Alger; the *Selected Poems* of Rupert Brooke; *Androcles and the Lion*, by Bernard Shaw; *The Case of the Velvet Claws*, by Erle Stanley Gardner. In those days he read confessions and movie fan magazines in precisely the same spirit as he read Dostoevsky or Kafka. They were all of them windows through which to seek a clearer and broader view of the universe in which he found himself. Now the dust leaves black streaks on his hands and causes him to sneeze; the paper smells sourly of vegetable decay.

Shivering in his coat, he feels like a burglar—the more so as he opens the desk and pokes about among the papers it contains: pages torn from exercise books and covered in his own handwriting in ink or pencil.

He reads:

It is then right to say that what we do depends on what we are; but it is necessary to add also that we are, to a certain extent, what we do, and that we are creating ourselves continually.

That from a sheet headed *Henri Bergson* and this from a sheet headed *John Langdon-Davies*:

The Universe as we know it through the senses is not necessarily "reality," whatever meaning we give to that term; it is the model which the brain constructs because it is of greater help in our struggle for survival than any other model.

The papers put back and the desk closed, he lifts open the trunk and mentally catalogues its contents: a fedora hat, brown, with a tiny red feather in its wide, darker brown band (the only hat Kevin ever owned, and what a fine fellow he thought himself, lounging in front of the movie house in Windsor, with a cigarette in the corner of his mouth and that hat worn at such an angle that the brim almost touched his right eyebrow); a pair of khaki shorts and a single brown sneaker (discoloured by the sweat of the man now looking down at them); a T. Eaton Company

86

mouth organ; a Newfoundland one cent piece, a Westclox pocket watch without a stem; an autographed picture of Myron Healy, a character actor who invariably got shot to death before the end of the film ("with luck, laughs and prosperity to my friend, Kevin O'Brien"); a Confederate flag and a St. Christopher's medal (souvenirs of the Windsor Exhibition); and a cigarette lighter shaped like a bullet (a gift from Laura).

He takes the lighter in his hand and flicks the wheel with his thumb. It gives off dust instead of sparks. This is Aladdin's lamp, he thinks. If I flick the wheel again, Laura will appear. He smiles, remembering an article he read in which a Freudian psychologist maintained that what Aladdin really did was masturbate.

"I love you," he had said to Laura.

And, "You don't have to say that," she had answered, sensibly. . . .

The train had been like every other; the passengers included a soldier, a pair of nuns, a drunken man and a crying baby. The soldier slept, rising and falling in his sleep as a man on horseback rises and falls in the saddle. The nuns, Sisters of Charity, both of whom wore rimless glasses, sat segregated in their black robes. The drunken man talked loudly to his seatmate, a farmer in dairyman's overalls, telling him about the double-header between the Boston Red Sox and the Baltimore Orioles that he'd attended the previous weekend; it had been Old Timers' Day in Fenway Park, and Jimmy Foxx, the old double x, had been there, and Dom Dimaggio, the little professor, and Lefty Grove. The baby howled until its howl was like a live thing, a bird flying back and forth above the heads of the other passengers, and from time to time its mother got up and walked with it in the aisle, swaying, her face half-hidden by the howling, blue

blanket-wrapped bundle, patting it and murmuring,
"There, there now, there, there."

Kevin had bought two chokingly dry ham and cheese
sandwiches, two Cokes and two Crispy Crunch chocolate
bars, and they'd eaten and drunk, he and Laura, while the
landscape flashed past: telegraph poles, zig-zagging pole
fences, moist-looking meadows, grazing cattle, brooks,
gray barns, white houses and, once in a while, on the left,
a sliver of sea. They hadn't talked much, had said nothing
that two strangers thrown together by chance mightn't
have said. The strangeness of their situation made him
more than normally shy; once when the train rounded a
curve she was thrown against him, and he said, "Excuse
me; I'm sorry," and then felt ridiculous.

At Tarleton Junction they learned there would be no
train leaving for Boston until the following morning. So
they walked, carrying their bags, her black cardboard suitcase and his duffle bag, to what appeared to be the town's
only hotel. It was a fairly long walk and Kevin imagined
that many of the people they met on the street blinked at
them inquisitively. We must look like a couple of goddamn hicks, he thought, wishing he'd had sufficient sense
to hire one of the cabs that had been parked at the end of
the station platform. He was also ashamed that at the
station lunch counter he'd said, "No sugar, please," to the
waitress from whom they'd ordered coffee when, of course,
the sugar was there, almost in front of him, in a little dish
made with a kind of spout, and the waitress had nothing
whatever to do with it. "That guy said he didn't want
sugar," he overheard her telling the short-order cook. "So
what," the cook snapped. "Maybe he don't like sugar."
But he replied in that manner, Kevin knew, only because
he was overworked and annoyed with the waitress for
having the time to tell such little jokes. The worst of it was
that Kevin was aware that the waitress was amused not
so much by his ignorance as by his red-faced and, for an
instant, almost wild-eyed embarrassment.

When at length they found themselves alone in the
room with the coin-operated radio, the bed tables scarred

88

by cigarette burns, and the framed photogravure prints of Banff National Park, the Halifax citadel and a team of oxen standing under an apple tree in blossom, he felt an almost intoxicating sense of relief; it was as if they'd reached a sanctuary. "I wish we could stay here for ever and never go out," he said, seating himself on one of the twin beds and leaning back with his arms behind his head, so that he was half sitting and half lying down.

"God, you do have some morbid thoughts," Laura said. She was undressing. "The first thing I'm going to do is take a long, hot bath. I'm going to soak until my skin wrinkles. That train was like a pigpen. I feel greasy all over." He shifted his eyes as she slipped out of her underpants. "Oh, darling, you are funny," she said. Her voice was amused, but tender; it was as though he heard, rather than saw, her smile.

"Bitch," he said, reaching out for her.

"Not now," she said, pulling away. "Later." She went into the bathroom, naked except for her sandals. Moments later he heard her urinating. He winced. Why hadn't she shut the door? Then he was angry with himself for being so fastidious, another Jonathan Swift. Still, weren't women supposed to have a greater sense of delicacy? He heard her flush the toilet and turn on the tub. "Balls," she said, "the damn water's the colour of mud."

They had met six months earlier. "Somebody's movin' onto the old Pratt place," Kevin's father had said. "You best take a hike over there and see if you can give them a lift." So Kevin had got on his bicycle and ridden down the road to the old Pratt place, which to a stranger would have looked no different from a dozen other farms in the settlement. This was thin-soil country and many of the farms were no longer worked. The Pratt place was a whitewashed wood frame house with lightning rods on its roof; an unmown yard; a sway-backed barn topped by a weather vane carved in the shape of a rooster; apple trees, rose bushes and a rhubarb patch, all of them running wild; and a rusted horse rake abandoned in a field.

There had been nothing much for Kevin to do there. In

such a situation there was no one to give orders, and he was too shy to volunteer, so he either stood out of the way, feeling stupid and superfluous, or struggled to find room to take hold of a stove or sofa that was already in motion, with more than enough men to carry it. How he envied the men who devised ingenious methods of putting long-legged tables through narrow doorways or found the rollers and burlap needed to move a stove without scratching a hardwood floor!

"You look the way I feel," Laura had said. Her long black hair was tied up in a pirate chief kind of kerchief. She wore a red blouse, its tails knotted at her waist, and tight blue jeans streaked with dust. She was laughing at him, and being laughed at usually filled him with a rage that was almost epileptic in its intensity. But this time it was different: he laughed with her.

"I live up the road aways," he said. My name's Kevin O'Brien. Most people call me Kev."

"Hello, Mr. Kevin O'Brien," she said. He glanced down at her feet, which were bare; there were bits of pink polish on her toenails. "I know," she laughed. "I look godawful."

"What? No, that wasn't what I was thinking. You look great. Just great."

"You're sweet," she said. "You're a terrible liar, but you're sweet. I'm Laura. We're going to live here in Dracula's Castle. That's my lord and master standing over there between the three-legged table and the easy chair that looks as if it were moulting."

He had already met Peter Trenholm. "How are you doin', kid," the man had said. He had red hair and his arms were so freckled that the skin was almost solidly orange.

"Let's go some place where we can take a load off our feet," she said. "They'll never miss us."

He followed her around the house, away from the others. They sat down on the back steps and looked out over the fields, toward the woods. The sound of men talking and moving furniture seemed to come from very far away. "God," she said, "it's so desolate. The grass. And the wind. How do people keep from going crazy?"

90

"Some of them don't," he said. "No, it's not all that bad. Not really. Not when you get used to it." He wondered what she would say if he confessed that he found it beautiful.

Several weeks later he had admitted it. And she merely smiled. "How many other places have you been?" she said.

"I've never been anywhere," he said bitterly, as though acknowledging a weakness for which there was no hope of remedy.

She patted his cheek. "Poor old Kevin. Don't take it so hard. You've got all the time in the world. You're just a kid."

"I'm not a kid," he said. "I'm eighteen."

"Liar," she said.

"I was seventeen in January."

Soon he was showing her his watercolours and talking to her about the books he borrowed each Saturday from the regional library in Windsor. "Listen to this, Laura," he would say. " 'Your joy is your sorrow unmasked. And the selfsame well from which your laughter rises is oftentimes filled with your tears.' That's from *The Prophet* by Kahlil Gibran. He came from Lebanon. Isn't it great?"

He tried to teach her to play chess, and she tried to teach him to play the guitar. They went bicycling together, like children, and they listened to her collection of records. His favourites were Nat King Cole singing "Lavender Green," and Fats Domino singing "Blueberry Hill." He also liked *The Third Man* theme.

Peter was an NCO with the permanent militia in Halifax, home only during the weekends. But his great dream was to be a farmer. A farmer was his own boss, Peter said, and didn't have to take orders from anybody. On Saturdays and Sundays he worked at repairing the barn; or he thinned carrots which he intended to sell to a wholesaler in Windsor; or he mended fences, stripping to his army boots and khaki shorts and pounding the posts into the ground with a sledge hammer. He talked of buying hens; there was going to be big money in poultry, he said.

"He's a worker," Kevin's father said, awarding his

highest compliment. "But that woman of his—well, it's none of my business."

"Pete doesn't know what it's like for me, being shut up here," Laura said to Kevin one evening as he prepared to go home. "It's like being in prison, in solitary confinement. If it wasn't for you, Kevin, I really would go crazy."

He kissed her. It was a very cautious kiss and in bestowing it he stepped on her foot. "Ouch," she said.

"I'm sorry," he said. "I'm a damn fool. Somebody should take me out and shoot me."

"Poor Kevin," she said. "Poor old Kevin." They were standing in the centre of the living room. She pressed her mouth hard against his, and kept it there; her hand reached under his shirt and began stroking the small of his back.

He drew back his head a little. "Laura," he said, "Laura, I love you."

She put her index finger on his lips. "Don't be silly," she said. "You don't have to say that."

"But it's true," he said. "I do love you." He laid his hand on her buttocks, half-expecting her to push it away. Instead she used her free hand to unzipper her jeans. "Put it in," she murmured when he hesitated. "Your hand. Put it into my pants. Now the other side. Farther down. There. That's right. Do you like that?"

"Jesus," he said. "Jesus."

She laughed. "Let go of me a second." Very quickly she took off her blouse, jeans and brassiere. "Damn," she said. "I better lock the door."

He almost wished he could go home now and think about what had happened. It was pride rather than desire that kept him from mumbling stupidly, "It's late; I'd better be going."

"Hurry up," she said to him when she came back.

"What?"

"Hurry up and strip. You want to, don't you?" This was not the way it happened in the sex manuals; there girls were timid and had to be aroused gently.

"Sure," he said. As he unbuttoned his shirt he tried to

recall whether his underwear was clean. Then he thought how his Aunt Lorna was always telling him never to leave the house in dirty underwear: a person never knew what might happen, she said. He almost giggled.

Naked, he avoided looking down at himself, and scarcely looked at her. "Come here," she said. She kicked off her sandals and stood naked except for her underpants. He went to her. "Now. Take off my panties. No. Slowly. Very slowly. Here. Put your hands there. Both hands. Flat. That's it. Now. Press down. Not so hard. Slowly. That's it. Peel me."

That had been the beginning of the series of events that led to their arrival at this hotel. They were off to Boston with the two hundred and seventeen dollars and fifty cents that Kevin had saved that summer while shovelling gravel for the provincial department of highways.

Off to Boston in the green, in the green. Good old Boston, the home of the bean and the cod. In the Yewnited States of Amerikay.

He glanced through a leaflet that had been left on the bedside table. It informed him that Tarleton Junction had been the site of an eighteenth-century battle between the British and a party of French and Indians led by Coulon de Villiers, who later defeated George Washington at Fort Necessity. The town was the rubber boot capital and transportation hub of eastern Canada, the leaflet boasted.

"Hungry?" Laura asked when she came out of the bathroom. "I could eat a horse."

"We're getting to be just like two old married people," he said, grinning at her.

"Well, you can't eat the other thing," Laura replied.

By now it was dark. They ate in a Chinese restaurant where the single waitress wore bedroom slippers and chewed on a toothpick, causing them to giggle like exhausted children. Laura ordered egg rolls and a steak with soya sauce and green peppers, and Kevin, who had never before tasted either dish, said simply, "The same." There was a pinball machine which they played while waiting for their food, and a jukebox on which Eddy Arnold, the

Tennessee ploughboy, sang about a roomful of roses. They drank beer until all the hard edges became soft, smooth and round.

"I can just hear the old man," Kevin said, wiping foam from his lips with the back of his hand. "He's saying, 'I knew it, I knew it all along; I made me a half-wit when I made that one'."

"I don't suppose Pete's even noticed that I'm gone," Laura said. "Two or three weeks from now somebody will ask him where his wife is, and he'll look up from whatever it is he's doing, swilling the pig or poisoning the potato bugs—he'll look up from whatever he's doing and say, 'Huh, what's that you said? Why, I hadn't noticed, but I guess she is gone, now that you mention it'."

She laughed loudly. "People are looking at us," Kevin said.

"Let them look, for God's sake. We own as much of the world as they do."

The jukebox was playing "Rambling Rose." Their knees touched under the table. She smelled of the eau de cologne he had bought for her. "Look at the label," he had said. "It's the only real cologne there is. The others are just imitations. This is made in Cologne, the city of Cologne, in Germany."

"It's not too late for you to go back," she said.

"Why in hell would I want to go back?"

"You're just a kid, Kevin. Remember I'm seven years older than you are."

"Six," he said. "Look, do we have to go over all that again? It makes me itch. Tomorrow night this time we'll be in Boston."

"Where the streets are paved with gold," she said. "Poor old Kevin."

He finished his beer. "Let's do something," he said. "Even if we just go to a movie."

"Okay," she said.

Ray Milland and Lana Turner had murdered Lana Turner's husband; Ray Milland had loaded the victim's body into the trunk of his car and was driving into the

94

country, where he intended to abandon it. But he needed transportation back; so Lana Turner was following him in a second car. She had never learned to drive. She didn't know how to turn on the windshield wipers. It began to rain. . . .

Afterwards they stopped for hamburgers and more beer, and then returned to the hotel.

At one point, Kevin said to her, "Did I ever tell you about the weird daydream I used to have about running away?"

"No," she said, "I don't think so." She sounded weary.

"It was like being born all over again," Kevin said. "I'd leave everything behind, you see. Everything. I'd leave the house late at night after everybody was asleep—I never really did this but it's what I used to tell myself I was going to do—I'd leave the house after everybody in the village was asleep. Stark naked. The way I came into the world. With nothing. I'd leave my name behind, too. I wouldn't be Kevin O'Brien any more. I even used to wish I could take the fillings out of my teeth and leave them behind me. I'd go somewhere else and be somebody new."

He laughed. "I even thought out the details; I was going to climb into a truck while the driver was having lunch. Little Orphan Annie was always doing that, and it always worked for her." He laughed again. "The truck wouldn't stop again until it got to, oh, I don't know, Arizona maybe, or British Columbia, and then I'd get out without being seen, and maybe steal some clothes off a clothesline or break into a clothing store."

"Poor Kevin," she said.

"I wish you'd stop saying that."

"I'm sorry," she said.

"It's okay. I'm sorry I snapped at you. I'm just tired, I guess."

"It's the beer."

They undressed and made love and almost immediately afterwards he fell asleep.

He dreamt they had missed the train and were running after it, down the tracks, shouting for it to stop. He dreamt they boarded the train and discovered it was not a train but a roller-coaster, and the car in which they sat also contained a fully decorated Christmas tree and a coffin.

He was awakened next morning by the sound of bells. He had forgotten that today was Sunday. "What time is it?" he said. Then he realized that the other bed was empty.

"Laura?" he called. The bathroom door was open; he got up and looked inside, although it was obvious that no one was there.

Perhaps she was teasing him. Feeling an utter fool, he actually looked under the beds and in the closets.

Her suitcase was gone.

He sat down. Then he got up again and made another search of the room, this time looking for the suitcase. No doubt she had moved it when she dressed. How Laura would laugh at him when he confessed that for a little while he had been afraid that she. . . . He saw the note lying on the chest of drawers, in front of the mirror.

It was written in pencil on a sheet of paper headed *Royal Hotel, Tarleton Junction, Transportation Hub of Eastern Canada,* and it read: *Kevin I'm sorry Laura.*

His mind wouldn't tell his body how to react; for a long moment he did nothing. Then he laughed.

He laughed again when he found that she had taken five twenty-dollar bills from his pocketbook.

He lay down, buried his face in the pillows and cried a little.

He rolled over on his back, dried his eyes on a corner of a pillowcase, and laughed again.

It didn't occur to him to go looking for her, although he realized she might still be at the railway station. He lay on the bed all morning, not so much thinking as waiting for some thoughts to come. At noon he discovered to his surprise that he was hungry.

an act of
contrition

Judd has awakened, Kevin has come downstairs; they have
had another drink together. Now Judd is preparing their
dinner of tea, canned salmon, canned peas and potatoes,
while Kevin again experiences that sense of guilt peculiar
to the escapee—the passenger who did not go down with
the ship, the prisoner whose death sentence was commuted
on the night that his companion was hanged, the O'Brien
who did not live out his life as a work beast in Lockhartville.

"Kathleen has been writing to me again," he says at last.
Kathleen is his father's sister.

Judd snorts almost inaudibly, smiles a little, rueful smile
and slightly shakes his head. Kevin realizes for the first
time that this combination of gestures is characteristic of
both him and his father. And more than likely—so he
reflects—it was also characteristic of his grandfather, and
would be characteristic of his son: each time a man snaps
his fingers or crosses his legs in a certain way he exercises
a small part of his ancestral legacy.

"I hope you wasn't fool enough to write her back," Judd
says.

"No, I didn't. But I kept thinking that I should have."

"She's crazy as the birds," Judd says. "As odd as the
hills. I wouldn't pay no attention to her if I was you."

But of course Kevin already has paid attention to her.
Not in a way that will help her but in a way that he hopes
may be helpful to him, in exorcising the ghosts and
expiating the guilt that raised them. He has, in truth,
answered her letter, although the answer is not one that
he could ever send to her. It, too, lies among the contents
of his briefcase:

Today at the office there was another letter from my father's sister Kathleen, the sixth that I've received from her in the past two weeks. She writes from the bottom to the top of the page as well as from left to right, as was often done in the eighteenth century, the lines of script criss-crossing, and refers to persons unknown to me with a third person pronoun and no further identification. "He says you make newspapers and are rich man. She says you should help me." The letters are written in pencil, each of them filling one double sheet from the centre of one of those blue-lined, two-by-five-inch notebooks. The envelopes are addressed in ballpoint ink and in another, much more legible hand. "Help me," she writes. "I need coat. I need shoes. I need medicine. I am old. Help me." *Help* is one of the words that convey a special meaning, not to be found in any dictionary, in the dialect of that part of Nova Scotia where I was born and grew up. As a small child I asked somebody what a mayor was, and was told that he was the man to whom you went when you needed *help* from the town. I didn't have to be told that *help* in this instance meant not comfort or advice but goods or money that, at least in the opinion of the recipient, were not so much given as shared. In those days in small towns one went to the mayor to apply for the dole.

It has been twenty years or more since I last saw or heard from Kathleen. At that time I worked occasionally for a neighbour who owned an old truck in which we hauled edgings from the sawmill in our village to Halifax, where he sold them for firewood. With the money he made from the wood he bought rum and beer which he later bootlegged, at double its retail price, to the mill workers. During one such trip Kathleen and I encountered one another accidentally on the street near the Lord Nelson Hotel. She wore a red beret and a red cloth coat over her black and white housemaid's uniform and when she kissed me I smelled her distinctive scent, at once medicinal and unclean, an interfusion of antiseptics, face powder and lipstick. "You're a man now, Kev," she said. "And you're so big! I bet you can make the little girls squeak." Her laughter, as always, was a dog's yelp of pain. I suppose passers-by must have stared at us and snickered; I was too embarrassed to look. "I've started goin' to a different doctor," she said. "That Dr. Cohen's wife, she got jealous of me." Before the conversation ended she asked me if I could lend her five dollars. "Mama was always good to you, Kev; she took care of you after your own mother left you." I dug two one-dollar bills out of a pocket of my jeans and gave them to her; that was all I had. "God bless you, Kev," she said. "I'll pray for you every night." Kathleen attended services at a Baptist church every Sunday and believed that Jesus, whom she called the Good Man in the Sky, was the only man who ever lived who was exactly six feet tall.

Our family, and the other families in our village, never used the word "friends." People were either *our own* which meant our relatives, or *strangers* which meant everybody else. And this usage prevailed even when the speaker despised or even hated the relatives in question and the *strangers* were old and intimate neighbours. At one point during the Depression, ten of our relatives, in addition to my parents and their three children, lived together in our house. Among them were Kathleen and her son Brady.

Small children don't normally distinguish what they've experienced from what they've been told. So while I re-member seeing Kathleen sitting on a kitchen chair inside the lilac bush with her son in her arms, that may have happened before I was born. There were two lilac bushes in front of our house, actually two thick clumps of bushes, each with its own character: we could have given them human names without feeling ridiculous, although we never did so. They'd not been trimmed since my father bought the place with money borrowed from a widowed sister's life insurance, and so they were at least eight feet tall at the centre. The one beside the driveway needn't concern us here. It was simply there, like one of those quiet, harmless people you meet and immediately afterwards forget. But the other, the one standing beside the path to the front door, was an intrusive but benevolent neighbour. I suspect that when we children picked lilacs we always, or almost always, took them from it. Inside there was a kind of grotto, a clearing in a miniature roofed forest, and when the bushes were in leaf or, best of all, in flower, you could pull certain branches apart and enter. When the branches swung together you were separated from the world in a place that was cool and dusky even on the brightest and hottest summer afternoons. The grotto provided almost exactly the same sensations as a total eclipse of the sun. These bushes, and an apple tree by the henhouse, outlived everything else planted by the previous owners, continuing to thrive long after the rhubarb, the hydrangea, the winterberries, and the white and pink roses had died from neglect.

"Poor little Brady," Kathleen always called him; and I tend to think of him as a babe-in-arms, although I've been told that he lived to be eight years old.

The father of her child hadn't wanted to marry her but had somehow been coerced into doing so. Nobody ever told me this, but as a little boy I overheard bits and pieces of a thousand conversations concerning it. The mind picked up two or three words and stored them until they could be attached to four or five words picked up somewhere else. *That son of a bitch . . . Pete Blair. . . . They were picking blueberries. . . . On the burnt ground. . . . He changed his tune . . . when he saw . . . we had the sheriff with us. . . .* The reason the baby wasn't normal, my grandmother said, was because Kathleen tried to kill it before it was born. One thing she did was climb up on the lumber piles behind the sawmill and jump off. The reason the child died, my father said, was because Kathleen wouldn't give it any peace; she'd never let go of it; she crushed it with her hugs and smothered it with her kisses. So that her love did what her hate had failed to do.

She and her husband never lived together, not even for

a day, but she called herself Mrs. Kathleen Blair and wore
a ring that she bought for less than a dollar; and it's more
than likely that, as has happened before in my native
village under similar circumstances, she'll one day be
buried beside him, with a single stone at the head of their
graves.

While she waited for the baby to be born, and again
while she waited for it to die, she made floor mats from
feed sacks and rags; hooked mats, they were called. Some
of the village women made mats depicting evergreen trees
or red and yellow roses; others divided their mats into
squares, like a checkerboard, or covered them with six-
pointed stars. Kathleen adhered to no pattern at all. When
I was so young that occasionally when there was nothing
else to do I simply stared at something for as long as I
could bear it, I found that if I stared long enough at
Kathleen's mats they frightened me, just as, if I stared
long enough into the face of a cat, I couldn't help laughing.

The distance between the rich and the poor is less than
the distance between the poor and the poverty-stricken.
The problem of the poor is that they lack money, while to
the poverty-stricken the lack of money is almost irrelevant,
in the sense that the cause of his disease is almost irrelevant
to the victim of cancer.

When I was a very little boy, Kathleen made false teeth
from sealing wax and wore them in her mouth. She and
my grandmother then lived in a separate part of our house,
and she must have been in the habit of entering and searching my parents' quarters while they were away from home,
for when we went out for a walk on Sunday my mother
and father would leave by a window instead of a door. I
remember them lifting my sister Stephanie and me over
the sill, and whispering to us to be quiet so that Kathleen
wouldn't hear us. I loved that.

Like everyone else in our family she played the mouth
organ; and she used to sing a song containing the words,
"Oh, never marry an old man, I'll tell you the reason why."
After she moved to Halifax, where at first she worked in a
restaurant, my grandmother occasionally took us to spend

the weekend with her in her furnished room. The two of them shared the bed, and Stephanie and I slept on the floor. I was almost equally fascinated by the flush toilet at the end of the dark brown and badly lighted hall and a reproduction of a painting entitled *Horse Fair* that I had to pass on my frequent trips to the bathroom.

I got acquainted with a girl about my own age, eleven, who lived in a big house about a block away from Kathleen's rooming house. Her name was Sandy and she was a day student at a private girls' school. I knew that because I'd asked her why she was dressed so funny, after I'd seen her once in her uniform of long black stockings, short pleated skirt and sailor's blouse.

Sandy and some other kids and I played games such as blindman's buff and puss-in-the-corner in the garage behind her house, until one Sunday afternoon when we were all of us delirious with excitement and yelling at the top of our voices, Sandy's mother appeared in the doorway. Even before she spoke we knew that something was very wrong, that she was in one of those mysterious and dangerous adult moods that even the least sensitive children instantly recognize. "I'm very sorry," she said to me with that cold, self-congratulatory politeness peculiar to certain middle class mothers. "I'm very sorry, but I'm afraid you'll have to leave." If I had been asked why it was that she was ordering me to go, I'd have answered truthfully that I didn't know. Yet the force of her convictions was so overpowering that I felt that I had, in fact, done something of which I ought to be ashamed. I stood there in my ragged sneakers and khaki shorts, prepared to plead guilty to whatever offence I was charged with. Moreover, I sensed that Sandy and the others were now viewing me through quite different eyes. For a moment they had been bewildered and a little scared, and then instinctively they had united behind the mother and against me. "Go to hell," I said, "the whole bunch of you," and ran out the door, past the woman on whose face there was now an almost gentle smile of mockery, and down the street.

Several years later Kathleen fell in love with Giovanni

Rocca. I'll never forget that name, because for more than a year, whenever she visited Lockhartville or we saw her in Halifax, she talked about nothing else. After he dropped her and took up with another woman, Kathleen kept going to his house every night and banging on the door, demanding to be let in. Finally, one night she threw a stone through the picture window of his front room, and he came out and broke her nose with his fist.

It was a God's blessing, the family agreed, when Kathleen became, first, a housemaid and, later, a cook for the Bannisters. During her twenty years with the Bannisters, she learned to cook not only in the French and English, but in the German and Italian manner; she had made dinner for a prime minister, sundry premiers, admirals and bishops, and a high commissioner, whom, to her immeasurable delight, was said to be a distant cousin to the Queen Mother. Yet she tasted the epicurean dishes that she prepared only when it was imperative that she do so, preferring to make her own meals from the foods she had eaten or, as often as not, gone without, during her childhood: buckwheat pancakes, turnip greens flavoured with salt pork, or salt herrings boiled in the same water with potatoes in their jackets. When certain of her adolescent nieces refused to recognize her on the street, as sometimes happened on Saturday nights when she walked downtown to listen to the Salvation Army Band and they, the nieces, came in from the country to dance or go to the films or to hear Hank Snow and the Rainbow Ranch Boys or Doc Williams and his Border Riders, she would shout after them, "Don't you forget, me girl, you was raised on bread and molasses the same as I was!" They would strain every muscle, then, in their efforts to shrink out of sight inside the hankie hats, sloppy sweaters, New Look skirts and bobby socks that were the fashion in those days. Because it *was* true that they, too, had eaten enormous quantities of homemade bread and Barbados molasses, sometimes with margarine, but more often without, and at that time, in that place, this was what you ate when there was nothing else (not even salt cod, onions and potatoes).

No doubt Kathleen's eating habits have provided her employers with another of what are referred to within the Bannister family as Kathleen Stories. "Our Kathleen," I can imagine Mrs. Bannister saying, "we love her dearly." Agatha Bannister is the granddaughter of an Anglican bishop who was famous in his day as a writer of animal stories; his obituary in *The Canadian Scribe and Bard* said that he possessed Kipling's genius without Kipling's vulgarity. She collects colonial furniture, of course, and is a sponsor of the Community Concerts Association. Her husband, Vincent, sat in the Nova Scotia legislature and served one term in the House of Commons before being appointed a county court judge. He has a theory, which he has expressed from the bench on any number of occasions, that there would be a good deal less juvenile delinquency if the inmates of reformatories were required to wear jackets and ties at mealtimes. When their son, Andrew, who is a surgeon in Montreal, visits his parents, Kathleen insists on making him at least one peanut butter and processed cheese sandwich—"for old time's sake, Mr. Andrew"—which she says he never refuses, although it's easy to imagine him saying, "Christ, sometimes it's hard to get rid of that godawful thing without the poor old girl knowing it." That's one Kathleen Story, I suppose. And there's probably another about how she began to prefer concert music to country and western music when the Bannister's daughter, Anna, started taking piano lessons. "That Anna, it's like she was my own," Kathleen always says.

It's more than probable that it was one of the Bannisters who found out the address of the newspaper for which I work and gave it to Kathleen. I suppose, for that matter, it was one of them who addressed her envelopes. "He says you make newspapers and are rich man. She says you should help me." But, alas, poor Kathleen, I don't have a pot to grow a geranium in, nor a window to show it out of.

I try to convince myself that I sympathize with Kathleen as I sympathize with the fat old charwoman I've often seen through my living room window climbing the hill past this apartment building after her day's work. The char-woman's legs are shaped like an elephant's; her ankles appear to be as thick as her thighs. She walks with the exaggerated purposefulness of a retarded child; although she stoops badly, she almost marches—almost goosesteps, in fact—bringing her feet down hard on the pavement, swinging her arms.

I long ago foreswore membership in the clan and com-mitted what used to be known in law as petty treason. I'd say that I have no regrets, if that weren't one of those affirmations that automatically negates itself. Perhaps it's true enough to say that I have regrets only when I contem-plate my reflection in another's eyes. For the next few seconds, ignore everything I've said and believe this instead: I come from a Haitian village and no fewer than six times in the past fourteen days I've found small clay and spittle images of myself on the front steps, each with a needle piercing its heart.

I could send Kathleen money for shoes, a coat, medicine; but I can't take care of her, I can't give her myself, which is what she's really asking of me. Certainly I can't give her the self that exists only in her imagination: the O'Brien boy, Kevin, who left home like the widow's son in the fairy tale, found a magic hollyhock that enabled him to turn stones into gold, and lived happily ever after. I swear that's how she thinks of me.

So I sit here, stupidly disgusted with myself for not being rich. For the first time in my life I regret that I've never made a great deal of money, as I have little doubt that I could have done, had I been willing to be other than what I am. This mood will pass, but at the moment I know in my heart that I owed that to Kathleen and the rest of them, the O'Briens and Foleys, my people.

night
watch

As always, when he is in Lockhartville, Kevin feels compelled to visit the sawmill. During his childhood and youth the mill absorbed so much of his life-essence in one way or another that its atmosphere is for ever an element in the climate of his mind. It is as if a part of him had been amputated and interred there, and that part contained nerves still capable of transmitting messages to his brain. This time he goes to the mill at night, carrying a flashlight that casts startlingly bright reflections on the steel saw blades, and finds to his satisfaction that no one else is there except the night watchman who lies asleep on an old car seat that has been converted into a sofa. He is glad that the night watchman is there, because the mill is a haunted place where he prefers not to be alone. He is equally glad that the night watchman is asleep.

A younger Kevin O'Brien was himself the night watchman in this mill. The Kevin O'Brien prowling about now with a flashlight, touching levers and examining the figures on gauges, noting that the water tank is only half full and the steam pressure has fallen to less than eighty pounds—that man would scarcely be surprised if at any moment he saw the young night watchman Kevin O'Brien walking toward him. So unnatural a sight might convince him that he had gone mad, but it would not surprise him.

Perhaps, the man thinks to himself, such a meeting has already taken place. I would not remember it, of course, because the Kevin O'Brien that I used to be would have no way of recognizing the Kevin O'Brien that I have become. He would see merely a stranger with a flashlight, and it is not uncommon for strangers with flashlights to visit the mill. What might he say to me, the boy that I was, if we met and were not too frightened to speak?

He could almost hear the voice of that other Kevin
O'Brien. . . .

Laugh as much as you like. This morning a
bird shit on my head. It made a sickening mess. I smell it
again each time I think about it, although I scrubbed until
my scalp burned and my arms ached. But that's not the
point. The point is it wouldn't have happened at all if
everybody didn't think I was some kind of half-wit.

It must have happened as I walked from the mill to the
cookhouse. Swallows build nests in the mill. It's beautiful
and a little weird to watch them fly in and out through the
open shutters while the saws and carriages make such a
racket that the trimmerman has to use sign language to
ask the tallyman, standing four feet away, for the loan of
his tobacco. The carriages rumble, the saws scream, but
the swallows don't seem to care. They fly back and forth
all day long.

At quarter-time, when the mill shuts down for oiling
and greasing, some of the guys make a game of throwing
board-ends at the nests. They giggle the way they did the
time they cornered the mouse in the bunkhouse and
capered around seeing which of them could stamp it to
death. The longer they chased it, the more they laughed,
until they were all of them staggering as if they were
drunk. The mouse kept running this way and that, dodging
their big boots, while they kicked at it or tried to jump on
it with both feet. Some of them grabbed sticks from the
box behind the stove and used them as clubs; and somebody was continually getting kicked in the shins, accidentally, or elbowed in the ribs, or was dancing up and
down on one foot after the other got clubbed—but that
didn't stop them from giggling. I don't know if they
succeeded in killing the mouse; I went outdoors as soon as

I could with the feeling in my head that you get in your stomach when you're trying hard not to throw up.

The nests are high, near the peak of the roof, and none of them has been hit yet. It's a damned shame, Hardscrabble says, their throwing things at the nests. What he actually says is: "The little birds, me boys. The little birds and the all-seeing eye of the great Calithumpian elephant! May he change you mean-arsed bastards into musical raisins!" Or something like that. But what he means is it's a damned shame. That's the way he talks when he's drunk. When he's sober he doesn't say anything.

The deal carrier, John the Hog, would have knocked down the nests with a smelt net if Hardscrabble hadn't bribed him with a pint of Lamb's Navy Rum.

But that's another story.

This morning a bird shit on my head and I didn't know it until all of us, about twenty men and boys, sat down to breakfast. I wasn't thinking about much of anything, just comfortably aware of how hungry and tired I was—unless the girl fever counts as thinking, and I don't suppose it does because it's always there, in the very front of my brain, just behind the eyeballs. My sister Stephanie has a friend, Barbara, and sometimes when she stays at our house overnight they wash one another's hair over the kitchen sink, neither of them wearing anything except panties and brassiere, and me sitting at the table pretending to read a book. And once, laughingly, they washed my hair, too, after I'd stripped down to my shorts. (I expect you realize that I'm lying to you now. They do wash each other's hair but before they come into the kitchen they put on their robes, and if they ever suggested that I undress I'd know they were poking fun at me, and tell them to go to hell. But sometimes what you imagine is more real than what's true.)

"Your hair," somebody said. I reached up and ran my hand through it. My fingers came away all filthy and stinking. And everybody laughed. The joke was I hadn't known.

John the Hog would have known. Bible Billy Bond

would have known. Even Hardscrabble would have known. But Kevin O'Brien hadn't known. He hadn't known because he was a fool, a simpleton, a moron, an idiot, an imbecile. And once he did know, he was too stupid to go wash himself and return to the table. He lurched to his feet, his cheeks and neck burning, and stumbled outside, into the millyard, followed by howls of laughter. And they would laugh harder when they realized that he was not coming back for his breakfast, the silly bastard.

What I'm telling you is that as soon as people decide that you're a fool all sorts of foolish things begin to happen to you. Things that wouldn't happen to anybody else, unless he too was a fool. I've already said you could laugh as much as you like.

Once when I was assigned to catch boards as they came out of the planer, I didn't lift one of them high enough and the end of it caught in the slab rollers behind me, without me knowing it. Someone shouted at me and although I couldn't make out what it was that he said I pretended, foolishly, that I could and shouted something back. He waved his arms wildly and I decided that he was trying to be funny, and so—like a fool—I laughed. Before I had sense enough to grasp what was taking place the board knocked over the long table of rollers, tearing out the spikes with which it was fastened to the floor, and sent me flying into a pile of sawdust and shavings. I must have looked like an imbecile lying there half-conscious, without the faintest idea what had happened to me—and of course it was inevitable that I would say something foolish. "Who hit me?" I asked.

Six or eight of us are walking across the lumberyard after a rain. All of a sudden, I hear the others laughing. I look around me. Stupidly. Everyone points at my feet. I've been wading in a porridge of red mud and foul green-black sawdust. My sneakers and socks are soaked through, and my feet are cold and slimy. Not one of the others stepped into this quagmire; they avoided it easily, probably without even being conscious of doing so, by simply moving a few feet to right or left. It was left for the idiot not only to step down into it, but to keep walking in it after any normal human would have felt the cold and the dampness, to keep walking in it until his footwear was ruined and there were blobs of filth between his toes.

My mind instructs my body to laugh or swear, but what comes out is not laughter or a curse but something between a squeal and a bleat. From now until the end of the summer anyone who can imitate that sound will be answered each time he does so by gales of laughter— although, strangely enough, there is almost always a certain furtiveness about such mockery. They will squeal or bleat at me only when I am a little distance away, or have left the room, so that I can pretend I haven't heard —and they can have the satisfaction of knowing that I have. I don't know why they should bother. Perhaps they're a little afraid of me? No, I can't really believe that. It's much more likely that mocking me when I'm almost out of earshot gives them greater pleasure than mocking me to my face; it makes them feel as though they've devised a joke that I'm too stupid to understand.

At this very moment I'm acting like a fool: nobody but a simpleton would make so much fuss about a mud puddle and a handful of birdshit. By understanding my problems I only add to them.

I'm night watchman at Hetherington's sawmill. The hours are long—from five-thirty in the afternoon until seven the following morning—but there's almost nothing to do between nine o'clock when I usually finish cleaning out the sawdust, and five o'clock when I have to start firing up the boiler. There's time to read and think.

To clean out the sawdust I use a broom, a shovel, a long rake with a rectangular wooden blade instead of tines, and a wheel-barrow. I call it sawdust for the sake of simplicity; actually the day's debris consists mostly of bark and bits of wood: board-ends and edgings. It has to be gathered up and piled in a corner where the next morning it's picked up and carried away in a horse-drawn dump-cart.

Summer nights are cool this close to the Atlantic. I've laid a twenty-four-inch-wide plank between two beams over the boiler and about thirty feet above the floor. Like a footbridge in a Tarzan movie. There's a ladder up the side of the boiler; I climb it and then walk out on a beam to the plank, where I put my jacket under my head and lie down. It's the only warm spot in the mill. I was comfortable enough there even in February and March, although the mill doesn't have any real walls: it's just a sort of big tent-like roof resting on a wooden frame.

I lie there in a little pocket of light from a coal oil lantern and read all sorts of things: Poe, De Maupassant, Lawrence, *The Psychology of Sex*, *The Story of Philosophy*, *Modern Screen*, *True Romances*, *Time*, Ellery Queen. Or I listen to the radio, mostly light classical music from WQXR. Or I think about girls. I have a photograph I cut out of *Life* showing three girls standing on a porch overlooking a beach with their backs to the camera and wearing nothing but their panties. The picture was accompanied by a story headed *Fashions*, and it said that red, yellow and blue panties like those worn by the three girls were beginning to be the style now.

I am more fascinated by the panties than by the girls, who would not interest me nearly so much if they were naked. Listen, I will tell you something that I have never told anyone else. I would kill myself if anyone else knew. One afternoon when I was alone in the house I went into my sister Stephanie's room and changed from my clothes into hers. Everything fitted me except her shoes which were painfully tight although I was able to get them on. It was very strange and exciting to stand there in one of Stephanie's frocks, and I thought how naked girls must feel in their skirts with their bare legs touching each other and the air circulating around their thighs, cooling the skin. Since then I have wished often that I were a girl, and beautiful. Because then, perhaps, I would not be expected to *do* anything. I could simply relax and let things happen to me. And that would be so much easier.

At about two o'clock I eat the lunch prepared for me earlier by Morgan, the cook. Strong black tea, biscuits, a

wedge of cheddar cheese, thick slice of cold roast beef or
a couple of hard boiled eggs. When I left home and went
to work my father said to me, "Never send anything back
to the cookhouse; they'll give you that much less the next
day and chances are you'll be hungrier." So if there's more
than I can eat I throw it in the furnace under the boiler.
Morgan is a Communist who predicts he'll live to see
Stanley Hetherington hang as an enemy of the working
class. He wraps my lunch in copies of the *Daily Worker*,
and has lent me pamphlets with titles like *The Mistakes of
Moses* and *One Thousand Absurdities in the Bible.*

We talk sometimes, Morgan and I, especially on Saturdays when the camp is almost deserted because almost
everybody has gone home, or into town to get drunk.
Morgan doesn't think I'm a fool, but that's only because he
doesn't think about me at all. I'm just an excuse for him
to talk to himself. The men ridicule him behind his back,
but are careful what they say to his face, knowing he
could put them on a diet of weak tea, stale bread and sour
beans.

"I used to think that our ruling class wasn't quite as bad
as the others," Morgan says. "That was before they
murdered Sacco and Vanzetti. When they killed those two
men I knew I'd been a fool. I'll tell you about Sacco and
Vanzetti some day. They were good men. Working men.
And the capitalists murdered them in cold blood. Oh, let
me tell you, there's nothing they won't do to keep their
money and their power. But our day is coming. I still hope
to be on the barricades before I die."

The four freaks here are Hardscrabble, Morgan, Bible
Billy Bond, and me.

About once a week Hardscrabble gets drunk and stays
in the mill with me all night.

"My father-in-law was a Freemason," he'll whisper
moistly. "And my youngest son . . ."—here he'll screw shut
his eyes and roar, his head vibrating like a child's top
when its spring is almost run down—"and my youngest
son is no son of mine at all . . ."—again his voice will drop
—"but the son of the Black Gillis, that Scotch Jew lawyer

who'd skin a louse for its hide and tallow, who'd steal the coppers off a dead nigger's eyes."

He slides his hand under the bib of his overalls and into the breast of his underwear. There's a legend about Hardscrabble's underwear. It's said he owns two pairs, and when he changes them he simply kicks the pair that he's taken off under his bunk, and leaves them there until he decides to change again. Now his hand comes out holding a bottle of whatever he happens to be drinking: rum, whisky, gin, vodka, hair tonic, shaving lotion or cake flavouring extract. "Are you a Doukhobor?" he asked me one night. "If you was to tell me you was a Doukhobor I'd have to kill you."

"Look out. If you don't watch yourself you're going to spill that all over yourself, and knock the lantern over besides."

"I killed me a Doukhobor once. Hell, I killed me a hundred of them. I was in the war, I was. The old war. The war with the Doukhobors."

"Where was that, Hardscrabble?"

"Don't you know nothin', boy? In Africa. In Africa. The Doukhobors, they was out to conquer the world. But we beat 'em, by God we did, and by the Lord whistlin' Billy-Jesus, if we have to, we'll beat 'em again!"

I wonder if Hardscrabble is like me: caught inside his own skull like a lightning bug in a jam jar. Or maybe the real Hardscrabble and the real Kevin O'Brien are only two inches tall. Maybe what we call our bodies are not our real bodies at all, but robots, and there's a control room inside my head where the little man who is the real me works levers and presses buttons to make me walk and talk. And maybe something's gone wrong with the machinery so that when the real Kevin throws the switch that ought to make the robot say "yes," the mechanical mouth says "yea-huh" instead.

There was no fork beside my plate, only a knife and a soup spoon. I knew I'd make a fool of myself if I asked for one. "Hey, Morg, how about a fork?" I'd say. Or, "Morgan, I don't seem to have any fork." Or "It looks as

114

if we're short of forks, Morg." But, of course, I'd mumble
it all except the single syllable "fork" which I'd croak or
squeak. Or it might even be "ork" or "urk" or even "oink."
Yes, it was sure to be "oink." And ever afterwards anyone
who wanted a fork would call loudly for an "oink." It
might even become my nickname.

So I said nothing, and ate my meat with a spoon—and
of course everyone noticed what I was doing, and of course
nobody eats his meat with a spoon unless he's a fool.

Behind the mill, and separated from it by cedars and
alders, are the sawdust piles, the accumulated sawdust of
fifty years, great dunes of sawdust that become by moonlight a desert on the moon. I stand there sometimes looking
up at the moon and imagining that it is the planet Earth.
Yellow moonlight on yellow sawdust. The shadows of
trees. My own shadow which does not even vaguely
resemble that of a man, or anything human. There are
moments when I'd like to run naked across the surface of
the moon.

What would they do to me, the others, if they found me
out?

And what would they do to me if they knew I was afraid
of the dark, although less afraid of it than of them?

They would put me in a dark room, and lock the door,
and go away and leave me there.

I've made up a story in which a man and a woman have
a baby which they keep in a windowless room. When it
begins to understand what is being said to it they tell it
that it is God. The baby grows into a child. "You are
God," the parents keep telling him. There is nobody to
contradict them, nothing, except perhaps a voice in the
child's mind, and if he hears such a voice, they tell him
that it is the devil, tempting him. So he grows up and one
day the doors are thrown open and, for the first time, he
goes out into the world, of which he has been taught to
believe that he is God. . . .

I'm not sure what happens then. But I suspect that he
has only to stretch out his hand to raise the dead.

115

the
hetherington
murder
case

I was born of slaves, thinks Kevin O'Brien as he drives
away from the mill, I was born of slaves and because the
brand of slavery is burnt into my flesh I have been prey
to dreams in which I could be omnipotent. But I am putting
that behind me now; I am squeezing the slave from my
ego and need no longer play at being lord of the universe.
The mind digests experience as the body digests food,
transforming a part of it into flesh and blood and bone, and
a part of it into urine and excrement. But, unlike the body,
the mind has no permanent mechanism to distinguish
quickly between what ought to be assimilated and what
ought to be evacuated: often it rejects the nutrients and
absorbs the wastes. Kevin is reminded of Yeats' poem containing the words, "The foul rag and bone shop of the
heart."

And what about the writings that he carries with him?
How much of the material in his briefcase is sewage?
(A dangerous question, that, interjects the voice of Kevin
Sardonicus.) One day a year or five years from now he
will reread one of those manuscripts—if by then they
haven't all of them been destroyed or hopelessly lost—
and more likely than not he will wince with embarrassment, thinking: What garbage this is! What a clumsy liar I
am! Those people weren't like that; Kevin O'Brien was
never like that; that wasn't at all the way that it happened.

Take for instance the manuscript that he has entitled
The Hetherington Murder Case. The incident with which
it ends is a lie; Kevin O'Brien was never able to smile at
Stanley Hetherington, indulgently or otherwise, and cer-
tainly he was never crazy enough to return a pay cheque.
In reality, the day that he was fired he crept away like a

117

pup that has been punished for dirtying the floor—but he went back later and did to Hetherington what he had for so long intended to do.

Which is to say that he killed him and hid the body so cunningly that it has never been found.

Kevin O'Brien hated Stanley Hetherington. But his hatred was cranial rather than visceral—his guts persisted in submitting to the man in a way that was almost filial. He knew, to his disgust, that Hetherington could have commanded his affection—yes, affection—if he had thought it worth a snap of his fingers. For Kevin had been taught all his life that the Hetheringtons had a right to his respect. They were the owners of the sawmill, which meant that in effect they were the owners of the village. Kevin's father had worked for Stanley Hetherington's father, and Kevin's grandfather had worked for Stanley Hetherington's grandfather, and when he was fourteen years old Kevin had been taken out of school and put to work for Stanley Hetherington. That had seemed perfectly natural to him. He had great and secret ambitions. He planned on being a famous and wealthy author and the lover of film stars, but that was in another world that existed in his imagination and in the endless future, like his earlier dreams of growing up to be a prophet or an emperor. That is not to say that he knew his aspirations to be fantasies; rather they existed on a different plane of reality in which they were so certain of fulfilment that it was as if they had already been achieved. So it was no defeat for him to go into the mill, and he might have remained there all his life, as his father had done, if it had not been for the plain fact that he was stupid and Stanley Hetherington was amused by his stupidity. "That lad hasn't got the sense that God gave to geese," Stanley Hetherington said of him; and it was true. But Hetherington did not fire him; he kept him as a court fool. And Kevin was too cowardly to quit, although the cowardice that was so much a part of his nature was not so much fear in the ordinary sense of the word as a kind of atrophy of the muscles of the will—he devoted such energy to his inner and secret life that he moved through the external world like a sleepwalker. Besides, even now that he was sixteen, servility was almost instinctive to him; the habit of obedience was in his blood. His customary reaction at this point in his life to almost any encounter with another human being was to blush furiously and mumble, "I'm sorry."

So he wished to murder Stanley Hetherington without actually killing him and there were various ways in which he might have accomplished this.

It is early morning and a young man in overalls is lying prone in the grass under the trees across the road from a large white house. There is little traffic and no other houses nearby. The young man has been waiting for several hours, having come here before daylight. Although it is summer the ground is damp and he is cold. Then the front door of the house is opened and a man steps outside, closes the door behind him, and starts down the walk toward the road. The young man tightens his grip on the object that rests on his forearm and against his shoulder. "Bang! You're dead," he mutters.

Or it is night and the same young man is crouching behind the rose bushes beside that same front door. Again, he has been waiting for a long time and it is wet and chilly. A car turns into the driveway and a man gets out of it. He is about to climb the front steps when a figure bounds out of the darkness and slams something hard and heavy against his chest, staggering him. "Die, you dog!" Kevin O'Brien bellows.

For an instant, Stanley Hetherington is speechless. Then, "You could have killed me," he says, his voice quavering.

"That's the general idea, you jerk," Kevin O'Brien replies.

119

"But why didn't you use a real knife?" Hetherington asks, his curiosity overcoming his terror.

"Because I don't want you to get it that quick," Kevin tells him. "Someday soon I'll do it again, and maybe next time the knife will be steel instead of wood. You won't know until it touches you. I may decide to do it over and over again the way I did it tonight, or I may get bored and finish you off tomorrow. You won't know what I've decided to do until it's too late. But one thing is certain, Hetherington, you stuttering creep, you're going to die, and I'm the man that's going to kill you."

No, that wouldn't do. There was the police. Worse, much worse, there was the strong possibility that Hetherington would merely laugh. "You'll never guess what that nutty O'Brien kid did last night," he would tell the men in the bunkhouse. "The silly bugger jumped out of the bushes at me and stabbed me with a toy knife. I guess he must have thought he was playing cowboys and Indians. And he must be damn near twenty years old. I swear to God the bastard doesn't know enough to come in out of the rain." For the rest of the summer, perhaps for the remainder of his life, Kevin's nickname would be Heap Big Chief, which would be abbreviated in time to the Heap or the Chief.

It was imperative that he convince himself, or at least that he half-convince himself, that the weapon would be real. There was a .22 calibre rifle and a 12-gauge shotgun in the kitchen at home, and a hunting knife with a deer-horn handle. The most reliable weapon was probably the shotgun; and the safest place to use it was probably the empty sawmill on a Sunday night; Hetherington almost always went there once or twice to see if there was any danger of fire. The next problem was how to dispose of the body.

Kevin did not greatly care if he was caught. Since he was still too young to believe that he would ever die, he rather liked the idea of being hanged, of shouting, "Hey, world, look at me" from the gallows. But his adolescent

120

sense of propriety made him feel obliged to do his best to avoid being found out. He had read a great many detective stories, and in detective stories the murder was merely the act that set the plot in motion; the story lay in the murderer's efforts to elude his pursuers. It seemed that when you committed murder it was part of the etiquette to devise a means of escaping punishment; it was as if this were a duty the murderer owed to society. So he considered cremating Hetherington's body in the wood furnace that provided the heat for the steam engine that ran the mill. But he was not at all sure that the doors were large enough, and he very much doubted that there would be sufficient time to reduce the bones to ashes. There was always the river, but there would be little point in that unless he could drown Hetherington instead of shooting or stabbing him, and he knew he had neither the will, the strength nor the ingenuity to manage that. For a while he contemplated digging a grave in advance of the murder, and if he had done so it might have become unnecessary for him to proceed farther. Each time that he saw his enemy he could have found comfort in the knowledge that his grave was in readiness. "I know something you don't know" is one of the most frightening things that one child can say to another.

Then again he wondered if it might be better to postpone his revenge until that future time when he would be omnipotent. Twenty years from now he towers over a slobbering wretch that once was Stanley Hetherington. The man is broken, stripped of everything, abandoned. His crimes have found him out so the only choice left to him is prison or suicide. "Why have you done this to me?" he whines. "Why? Why? Why?" And Kevin thrusts his face close to his, says, "Look at me, Stanley Hetherington, look at me carefully. Don't you recognize me now? Yes, it is I, Kevin O'Brien, who have brought you to this."

One Saturday night in town Kevin bought his first copy of a socialist magazine, printed in Cape Breton on four smudged newspaper pages and called *Coal and Steel*. He

121

had for several years been in the habit of writing letters to the editors of newspapers and magazines, chiefly because seeing his name in print reassured him that this entity Kevin O'Brien did in fact possess an independent existence and was not purely the product of his own imagination. When he was younger he had sometimes signed such letters as an officer of an organization that had being only in his mind; he had been co-chairman of the Maskwesinaan Road Improvement Association and executive secretary of the Friends of Republican Spain in North America and president of the Canadian Association for Puerto Rican Independence. In his scrapbrooks there were letters of acknowledgement from *Time* and *Reader's Digest* in which the latter titles were typewritten under his name. He had written to the *Free Press Weekly* in Winnipeg protesting Canada's involvement in the Korean War, and to the *Family Herald* in Montreal saying that Henry Wallace should be elected president of the United States, and these letters, unlike those to *Time* and *Reader's Digest*, actually had been published. He had no difficulty in convincing himself that he was angry about the Greek Civil War and disturbed by the latest palace revolt in Venezuela. This was partly swank and partly a fumbling attempt to maintain his faith that there must be more to the world than he had experienced in this village. Because he knew, although he could not as yet articulate this knowledge, that if he lost that faith there would cease to be any reason for him to keep in touch with reality.

So he wrote to *Coal and Steel*. It was a four-page letter in which, along with much else, he said that Socialists "should glory in their scarlet," a phrase that seemed to him to be both stirring and felicitous. He signed it *K. Michael O'Brien*, a usage that he regarded as elegant. The following month he found that it had been printed on the front page under a three-column heading that read, "Worker Correspondent Flays Warmongers." He sat down that same night and wrote a sequel. This time the editor sent him a reply in which he agreed with his opinions, complimented him on his style, and asked him if he would

be willing to sell subscriptions and collect signatures to a
petition being circulated by the Canadian Peace Congress.
The editor's letter began *Dear Comrade* and ended *Yours
for the revolution.* Kevin wrote again, but before his third
letter had time to reach its destination he received another
from the editor. This one was accompanied by a parcel
containing copies of the *Canadian Tribune,* the *National
Guardian,* and the London and New York editions of the
Daily Worker.

The editor wrote:

Dear Comrade:
   I regret very much to inform you that Coal
and Steel *has been forced to capitulate tem-
porarily to the dupes and lackeys of neo-
Fascism. We will be unable to publish your
second excellent letter in which you tell the
capitalist exploiters, their petit bourgeois
henchmen and lumpenproletariat hirelings
exactly where to get off. My little paper is
kaput—but it was only a single spark. Enough
sparks remain to ignite the fiery dawn of true
liberty, true equality, true fraternity and
true peace throughout the world. I trust that
you will continue to fan those sparks.*
              Yours for the revolution,
                Angus R. Cameron

So much for that. Two months passed. Then one day as
he came out of Vaughan's General Store, Kevin happened
to meet Hugh Macdonald, the district representative of
the department of agriculture, a kind of rural equivalent of
an Indian agent, who dutifully had taken an interest in
him, an interest that manifested itself largely in telling him,
periodically and rather absent-mindedly, that he ought
to go back to school. They mouthed the usual nothings for
a while and then Macdonald said, with his man-to-man
grin but coldly attentive eyes, "What's this they've been
telling me about you getting mixed up with the Commies?"

Kevin laughed. "We're going to raise the red flag on top

of the smokestack at the sawmill," he said. "That's the nearest thing in Lockhartville to the Winter Palace of the Czars." He knew about the Winter Palace and the Czars from books he had borrowed from the Public Library in town.

"Seriously, O'Brien . . ." Macdonald always addressed him by his surname; it was part of the man-to-man routine. "Seriously, O'Brien, a couple of Mounties called at my office the other day. I don't know how they found out I knew you. They asked me all kinds of questions. It seems they suspect that you're a practising Communist, a card-carrying member of the Labour Progressive party. Of course I told them there must be some mistake."

"I've been selling atomic secrets to the Russians for years," Kevin said. "I get them from listening to the talk in the Hetherington cookhouse."

Macdonald's grin vanished. "It's no laughing matter," he said. "It wouldn't look very damn good for me if word got back to the department that I'd been fraternizing with a Red." To Kevin's amazement the man's voice had become shrill and defiant. "They said you wrote something for a Commie paper and were trying to get people to sign some kind of Commie petition. I told them it must be somebody else with the same name as you."

"Thanks," Kevin said.

"All right," Macdonald said in the half-admonitory, half-apologetic tone of a parent who is in the process of ceasing to be angry with a child. "I know you're smart enough to realize that the very foundations of our way of life are threatened by the international Communist conspiracy. Have you read *Masters of Deceit* by J. Edgar Hoover? You ought to. I'll lend you my copy. I'll try to remember to bring it with me the next time I'm passing through Lockhartville. And there's another book, *I Was a Communist for the FBI*. The cold shivers ran up and down my spine as I read that one." Macdonald shook his head thoughtfully. "Well," he said, "I've got to get moving." He slapped Kevin's shoulder lightly. "You remember what I told you the last time I was talking to

124

you? Get that arse of yours back into school. Later maybe you could go to the Agricultural College in Truro. Think about it."

"Yeah," Kevin said, "I'll think about it."

"You do that—and for Christ's sake don't get mixed up with those goddamn Commies. They'd destroy you."

"So long," Kevin said, as Macdonald disappeared into the store.

Before the week was out, Kevin's father had also been questioned by the RCMP. "God, boy, why can't you be like other people? It wouldn't be too bad if you'd of stole something. That would make some sense. Can't you get it into that goddamn stupid head of yours that people like us should keep our mouths shut and our arses down?" So too had Mrs. Glendon, the librarian, an old English woman who had introduced him to the works of Shaw. "I told them where they could go in language from Wapping bordering on Limehouse." Kevin presumed the mail man had been questioned too, although he hadn't said so; he had simply stopped speaking.

Kevin waited for the police to call on him, but they never did. Like most of the inhabitants of Lockhartville he looked upon the police much as the people of a country that was conquered and annexed in their grandfathers' time might be expected to look upon an occupying army. In Lockhartville when mention was made of the state it was always in the third person. So the police were the agents of an alien power. As such they were regarded with something very much like awe. To threaten an enemy with the police was to curse him, in both the divine and profane senses of the word. It was a threat that was often made but almost never carried out.

The sawmill workers were paid every second Saturday. The men went to the office where the payroll had been prepared by Hetherington's wife. It was said that prior to his marriage Stanley Hetherington had never gone out with any women other than the successive teachers in the village school. There was a legend that out of deference to him the school trustees had hired only marriageable girls and had fired those of them who had failed to strike his fancy. Florence Hetherington had been one of the teachers. On the first payday following Kevin's conversation with Hugh Macdonald she did not speak to him as she handed him his cheque.

Stanley Hetherington was standing beside his wife's desk, wearing dungarees, a suede windbreaker and, incongruously, rimless glasses. There was a nervous tic under his eye. "I'd like to speak to you alone," he said to Kevin. "In the other room. It will only take a second." He went into the adjoining room and Kevin followed him. He shut the door. "I've got a damn good mind to kick the shit out of you," he said.

Hearing himself giggle, Kevin wished that he were dead.

"You'll laugh out of the other side of your mouth when they get you behind bars," Hetherington said. His voice was shaking. "The Mounties have got your number, boy. My God, if it was up to me, I'd stand you in front of a firing squad, the whole damn bunch of you Communists."

"I'm not a Communist," Kevin said meekly, and despised himself still more. Somebody ought to take a red hot poker, he thought, and burn a hole through my tongue.

"Well, you're through here, boy. You'll never work another day for the Hetheringtons, and if I was Judd O'Brien, I'd take a belt to you and beat the skin off your arse, as big as you are. Your old man must be wishing you'd been born dead."

Kevin perceived that Hetherington's hands were also shaking. For the first time he began to observe him closely. "Why, you're scared of me," he said, his astonishment at this discovery jerking the words out of him. "You're scared to death of me, and all I did, really, was write a letter to a newspaper." For an instant it seemed to him that he must simply have thought this. It was so incredible to hear himself saying such a thing aloud.

"Get out," Hetherington said. "Get to hell out of here before I do something I'll be sorry for."

"Sure." Kevin said. Then he did what he afterwards

knew to be a very foolish thing. He took his pay cheque out of his shirt pocket, wadded it up and tossed it at Hetherington's feet. "There," he said, "that's not enough to do me any good. Besides, you'll probably need it more than I will."

"You damn fool," Hetherington said. Kevin smiled at him, indulgently.

his
native
place

It is almost time to abandon the present tense. For Kevin
O'Brien, newspaper reporter, has driven back down those
roads where we first encountered him and has boarded an
Air Canada DC-8 and is flying out from between the covers
of this book. "Each of us should travel as far as he can into
the past," Santayana said, "since none of us knows how
far he will travel into the future." Kevin remembered that
quotation at the beginning of his journey, flying toward
Halifax, and he remembers it again now. (Which pleases
him as when, upon leaving a town or city, he keeps a
fetishistic promise to himself to take one last look at the
first object he saw upon his arrival there: a certain tree
or traffic light or store front or street sign.) His journey
has taken him through time as well as space, which is to
say that like all truly important journeys it has been
largely imaginary. Also, like other myths, it has contained
a large element of the ridiculous. Here he sits strapped
into an armchair that hurtles through the sky three or
more miles above Quebec. In a world where such experiences are so commonplace that the participants watch old
films to relieve their boredom, who could confidently
separate the dream from the reality or the absurd from the
sublime? He drinks his double gin and tonic and continues
to entertain the idiot child within him. The words of a
silly old song run through his mind as he thinks about the
dance that he attended on his third and last night in his
native place:

> Did you ever go into an Irishman's shanty,
> Where water was scarce and whiskey was
> plenty?

129

"How you making it, Kev?" Allister drawled, seizing Kevin's elbow instead of his hand in the front yard of the Farmers' Hall.

"How's she goin', Kev boy?" roared Colin, raising his fists and making a little half-turn from the waist like a boxer.

"It's good to see you, Allister," Kevin said. "And it's good to see you, Colin. It's been a long time."

And it *had* been a long time, so long that he had forgotten how, when his cousins or any of the young men of Lockhartville greeted one another, they invariably pretended they were about to wrestle or box.

There was a silence during which the three of them stamped on the frozen turf and clapped their gloved hands. The door of the hall, a whitewashed shingled building, opened and closed, sending forth the sound of a fiddle being played partly in the Irish and partly in the French-Canadian manner.

"Lord whistlin' Jesus, it's cold," Allister said. "We better drag our arses inside before we freeze our balls off."

"How's about a little taste first?" Colin asked, patting a pocket of his green and black mackinaw. "I'm that dry I'm spittin' dust."

"You don't have to twist my arm," Allister said.

"Sounds like a great idea," Kevin said. They went around the corner of the hall, out of the light from the 200-watt bulb above the door. Kevin observed that while his cousins' waists were still as slim as athletes' they had begun to stoop, so that their arms seemed unnaturally long.

He took a deep breath, held it, and drank from the pint bottle Colin had handed to him. The liquid was icy cold but so raw that it seemed momentarily to have been heated almost to the boiling-point. It tasted like cheap vodka laced with peppermint.

He drank deeply, knowing they were watching to see how well he drank. In Lockhartville, a man who could not drink was consigned to the same hell as the weakling, the coward, the cuckold and the castrato.

"The first time I ever got drunk on that stuff," Kevin said, "I was fifteen. Coming home from a dance. Walking. When it hit me, I lay down beside the road. I can remember that. It was a very clear night and there were millions and millions of stars. I lay there watching them spinning down the sky. At first I thought it must be the end of the world and then I thought that I was going to die."

Allister laughed, rubbing the mouth of the bottle with his mackinaw sleeve. "Over the lips and across the tongue, look out guts, here she comes." He swallowed about four ounces and passed the bottle back to Colin.

"It's good to be back," Kevin said. "It's good to be home."

"Down the dusty trail," Colin said. He performed the same little ritual with his sleeve, then drank and put the bottle back in his pocket. Kevin noticed that he wore a hunting knife on his belt. It was a very wide belt, decorated with glass diamonds, rubies and sapphires.

"Well, let's get the hell inside," Allister said. He grasped Kevin's shoulder and shook him. "You mind Estelle Blaine, Kev?"

Kevin looked blank for an instant before he recalled that in Lockhartville "mind" could be a synonym for "remember."

"Yes, sure," he said. "I think I remember her. Sure."

Allister and Colin hooted. "You should have seen her face when I told her you was comin' home," Colin said. "She started whimperin' like a bitch in heat."

"She can't be more than a kid," Kevin said. "Sixteen, maybe seventeen years old."

"Like hell," Colin said. "She's the same age as me if she's a day. That'd make her two years younger'n you."

"If they're big enough they're old enough," Allister announced solemnly. He and Colin laughed and threw punches at one another's heads.

Kevin felt childishly proud, entering the hall between his cousins. Sentimental slush, a part of him said. Shut up, you cynical bastard, another part of him answered. For five years he had been a reporter and editor on a daily newspaper in another province, but he liked to pretend sometimes that he was a displaced logger. Tonight he felt like one.

The music was provided by Tracy Devlin and His Green Valley Boys—Black Watch tartan shirts, string ties, a fiddle, two guitars and a bass. "Hey, Kevin, how's the boy?" Tracy bellowed.

"Walk 'er, boy! Walk 'er!" Colin roared back. Kevin did not recognize the tune they were playing, but he supposed it was either "The Devil's Dream," "The Mouth of the Tobique," "The Liverpool Hornpipe," "Lord Macdonald's Reel," or "The Irish Washerwoman." It was always one of those five tunes, it seemed, just as in the old days every ox in Nova Scotia was named either Buck, Brown, Broad, Bright, Star or Lion.

"Long time no see," they said. And, "Jesus, Kev boy, I ain't laid eyes on you since Adam was a pup." And, "Hello, Kev, you old bastard, how are you?" Not that they knew him. He had been scarcely more than a child when he left and this was his first visit in years.

But he was Judd and Leah O'Brien's boy, Kevin, grandson of Michael O'Brien, that damn fool Irishman who lost his farm during the Depression because he was off digging for Captain Kidd's treasure on Oak Island, and of Blind Andrew Foley, the Plymouth Brother, who lost his eyes in the mine.

He was Kevin, brother of Patrick, who was killed in the war, and of Stephanie, who married the minister and moved to the States, where it was said that she had left him to run away with a sailor. He was Kevin, cousin of Allister and Colin, cousin of Sean and Alex and John Allan, cousin of Eileen and Catherine and Anne, cousin of Mary Bill Clarke and Mary Tom Williamson.

There was a place for him here.

He relaxed his will and allowed himself to slip a little closer to drunkenness. The walls on two sides of the hall were lined with kitchen chairs on which mothers and grandmothers sat, tapping their toes in time to the music,

132

infants wrapped in blankets on their laps. Small boys and girls played tag around a wood stove made from a steel oil drum while their mothers, fathers, aunts, uncles and cousins danced together.

Old women he could not remember and children he had never met greeted him and called him "Kevin."

"I bet you don't remember me," a girl said to him.

Like most of the girls here, she looked more European than North American—more like a girl in Normandy or Derbyshire or Clare than like a girl in Montreal or New York.

"I'm Estelle Blaine."

"Sure, I remember you, Estelle," Kevin said.

"Colin said you was coming home for a visit." She stressed the final syllable of "coming." "Talking proper" they had called it when he was a child.

"Just for a few days," Kevin said. "But now that I'm here I wish that I could stay longer."

She wore a very short skirt and an almost transparent blouse. It was funny, and a little pathetic, Kevin reflected, that nowadays girls in places like Lockhartville adopted exotic fashions more rapidly than most of their contemporaries in the cities, simply because their chief contact with the outside world was through television and their conception of what was fashionable was based on what was worn by Racquel Welch on the Johnny Carson Show.

"It must seem awful boring to you after living in the city and all."

"Cities are pretty boring too, sometimes," he said. "Would you like to dance?" He took her hand. "I'm not sure I remember how to do this," he said. "It's been a long time."

> Did you ever go into an Irishman's shanty,
> Where water was scarce and whiskey was
> plenty?

It didn't matter if you couldn't dance. If you couldn't dance you shuffled.

Estelle smelled of Evening in Paris and Scope and Crest

and of Toni Home Permanent. Her breasts were very firm against the front of his sports shirt.

"Hey there, Kev boy, you be good!" Allister yelled. "And if you can't be good be careful."

"Don't do anythin' I wouldn't do!" Colin shouted.

Allister was somehow managing to dance with his wife, Laura, who looked to be at least seven months pregnant, while holding a hot dog in one hand and a bottle of Seven-Up in the other. Colin leaned against the wall like a man being frisked by the police. A laughing blonde stood between his outstretched arms.

> *Did you ever go into an Irishman's shanty,*
> *Where water was scarce and whiskey was*
>   *plenty?*

"What are you laughing at?" Estelle asked.

"Nothing," he told her.

"Hey, Tracy!" Colin roared. "Give us a waltz, God damn you!" He lurched into the centre of the floor, elbowing dancers aside, dragging the blonde behind him.

"Anythin' to keep the customers happy!" Tracy roared back. It was "The Tennessee Waltz," as Kevin had been almost certain it would be. "The Tennessee Waltz," with Tracy sounding almost like Eddy Arnold, just as when he sang "I've Been Everywhere, Man" he sounded almost like Hank Snow.

Almost inaudibly, Estelle sang with him. Then Tracy played and sang "The Waltz of the Wind." This time Kevin could not identify the accent and mannerisms. Roge Miller? Faron Young? Ferlin Huskey? Again Estelle sang with him, her eyes half-closed, smiling as though almost asleep.

Watching her, Kevin felt lonely for the first time since his arrival. He was relieved when the band broke into a reel.

> *Did you ever go into an Irishman's shanty,*
> *Where water was scarce and whiskey was*
>   *plenty?*

Allister gave a wild cry, half war whoop and half rebel yell, and began to step-dance; almost squatting, his arms pumping, the steel plates on the heels and toes of his logging boots turning the hall into a giant drum.

"That's it, Allister. Give us a step!" the crowd shouted. "Walk 'er, boy! Walk 'er!"

They drew back and formed a circle. Allister yelled again, dancing like a Cossack or a Highlander or a Sioux, leaping three feet off the floor, bending back like a Limbo dancer, knees opening and closing, hand slapping his thighs and chest.

"Walk 'er, boy! Walk 'er!"

It was wholly masculine, wholly egoistic. When, as sometimes happened, two men danced, facing one another, each of them danced alone, improvising his own wild choreography. It went on until they were almost exhausted.

"Walk 'er, boy! Walk 'er!"

It was the way his ancestors had danced, Kevin knew, before pouring out of their bogs and mountains with swords and daggers in their hands and weird Gaelic war cries on their lips. It was the way the warriors of Brian Boru must have danced before the Battle of Clontarf, where they defeated the Vikings.

"Walk 'er, boy! Walk 'er!"

Allister knew nothing about his ancestors. He was not interested in his own past, let alone the past of his race. If he had known what Kevin was thinking now he would have been bewildered, amused and probably a bit contemptuous. Yet he had worked for fifty hours this week, cutting pulpwood and pit props when it was twenty below zero and there was a wind from the north, and here he was, dancing like a warrior. What would an anthropologist make of that? Kevin wondered, grinning.

And when he was finished, partly with pride, partly in embarrassment, partly to convince everybody, including himself that he had not been in earnest, Allister struck his chest with both fists and bellowed.

"He's sure a wild man," Estelle said.

"He sure is," Kevin agreed.

135

A few minutes later he went outdoors with Allister and Colin again, holding his breath while he swallowed, and afterwards sucking in great draughts of freezing air. He wanted to be thoroughly drunk. If he got drunk enough, perhaps all of his inhibitions would be burnt away and he would become wholly one with these people—his people. He had begun to feel—sentimentally, drunkenly—that he had somehow betrayed them. It was a feeling that had come to him at intervals even when he was a boy and lived here.

"You can't fly on one wing," Allister said. And they all three drank again. Irrelevantly, Kevin thought how Re repented that he had created men and sent Sekhmet the Powerful against them. The goddess killed men and waded in their blood until Re repented and poured out seven thousand jars of red-coloured beer in her path. Believing it was blood, she waded into it, became drunken and stopped her slaughtering. And Noah, after the end of the world, got drunk, stripped naked and lay in his tent. Or did he dance?

"What in hell you laughin' at, you crazy bastard?" Colin demanded affectionately.

"Nothing," Kevin said.

"You better keep an eye on that D'Entremont feller," Colin said.

"What?" Kevin asked, bewildered, wondering if they had said something that he hadn't heard.

"D'Entremont," Colin said. "Big feelin' son of a bitch from Frenchman's Cross. You mind how them bastards was always hangin' around here, scoutin' for girls."

"Yes," Kevin said, "I remember."

"He's been givin' Estelle the eye all night," Allister said. "She's a pretty nice piece of stuff."

"He used to go with her a little," Colin said.

"Well, look, if she's his girl he can have her," Kevin said. "I'm not looking for any trouble. That's the last thing I want."

Their silence told him he had said the wrong thing.

136

"You won't have a hell of a lot to say about it if he takes the notion it's trouble he wants," Colin said.

"He's a mean bastard," Allister said. "Maybe you want I should take care of him for you."

"No," said Kevin quickly. "No, I don't want you to do that."

"We'll see there's fair play," Colin said. "We'll stand to your back."

There was another silence during which they watched him intently, waiting.

"I'm not looking for trouble," Kevin repeated. Allister and Colin glanced at one another but said nothing. Kevin took a deep breath. "I'm not looking for trouble," he said, "but I don't intend to run away from it, either."

Allister and Colin grinned. He was again their kinsman. "That's the stuff," Colin said. "There's never been a man come out of Frenchman's Cross that was fit to hold the coat of an O'Brien."

"Goddamn right," Allister said.

"There's one thing you want to watch out for," Colin said. "Son of a bitch carries a toad-stabber. You better borrow my knife."

Kevin laughed, half-believing it was a joke, half-pretending to believe it was a joke.

"I don't think I'll need any knife," he said, trying to make it sound like a boast.

"Well, if you change your mind, let me know," Colin said.

"Like I say, he's a mean bastard, that D'Entremont," Allister said. "He put a feller in hospital once with that knife of his. God's truth, he did."

"Let's have another drink," Kevin said. "Let's have another two drinks."

He was practically certain that his cousins were teasing him, testing him. In the real world men did not fight with knives. Knife fights occurred only in films starring Robert Mitchum and Lee Marvin. He almost wished that he had accepted Colin's offer. A small phoney part of him was thinking of how, when he returned to the city, he could tell his friends that in his native village he had gone to a dance where it was necessary for him to carry a knife. They wouldn't completely believe him, of course, but he would be very convincing, because it would almost be true.

"I was startin' to think you'd forgot about me," Estelle told him when he returned to her.

"You're very beautiful," Kevin said expansively. She giggled. "Stop that, for God's sake," he said. "When strangers tell you you're beautiful you're supposed to smile, just a little, not too much, and say, 'thank you.' Now. Let's try again. You're very beautiful." Again she giggled. "To hell with it," he said.

"Don't be mad at me," she said.

"I'm sorry," he said. "Let's dance."

> Did you ever go into an Irishman's shanty,
> Where water was scarce and whiskey was
> plenty?

Who was it Kierkegaard had loved for her "sweet futility"? The last fist fight I had I was wearing short pants, Kevin thought. When I was a child in this village we went to school in our bare feet. I limped all summer, every summer. Because of sharp stones and thorns and broken glass. How strange it sounded to say "my village." It was always Europeans who spoke of "my village."

"Always the start was the village." On the plane flying to Halifax he had read Oscar Handlin's *The Uprooted*. "Always the start was the village. . . . This was the fixed point by which he knew his position in the world and his relationship with all humanity. . . . No man, for instance, could live alone in the village. . . ."

> Did you ever go into an Irishman's shanty,
> Where water was scarce and whiskey was
> plenty?

"Estelle," he said, "I think I'm falling in love with you."

"It's the moonshine," she said. "I can smell it on your breath."

138

"Drunk on moonshine," he said. "A man who is drunk on moonshine is a lunatic."

"You're no lunatic," she said. "You're just a little tight, that's all."

He kissed her. The village would not approve. Better if he pinched her behind. He did that, too. Gently. Her hair tickled his cheek. "That's Bob D'Entremont your cousins are talkin' to," she said.

"What?" He had almost forgotten. D'Entremont was taller than either Allister or Colin, and like them he stooped, so that his arms appeared longer than they actually were. His hair was cut very short, in the military manner, and he wore a small military moustache.

"I suppose he was in the army," Kevin said.

"Huh? Oh. Yeah. In the Highlanders. In Germany."

Like all impoverished provinces—like Ireland, like Scotland, like the American Southland—this was a land of soldiers. Kevin himself, supposedly a pacifist, had once hitch-hiked to Halifax to enlist and been rejected because of his eyes.

"To hell with Bob D'Entremont," said Kevin. "It's Kevin O'Brien you're dancing with. Remember."

He wondered what Colin and Allister were saying to D'Entremont. Probably they were warning him not to make trouble. "If you start anythin' we'll sure as hell be the fellers that end it," he could imagine Allister saying. And, "Don't start somethin' unless you're damn certain you can finish it." D'Entremont was outside his territory. If he were sufficiently provoked he might come back next week with a half-dozen friends from his own village. But that was next week. And next week Kevin would be writing heads. "Government Agrees to Tariff Talks." Set in 42 Bodoni bold, centred on a three-column slug. "Middle East Crisis Worsens." Set in 48 Cheltenham bold for six columns reverse plate with arrow ends.

Kevin was elbowed so hard that he almost fell and pulled Estelle down with him.

"Who the hell do you think you're pushin' around?" Bob D'Entremont demanded. He was grinning. His brown eyes were bright.

139

"Pardon me," Kevin stammered. "I'm sorry." As soon
as the words were out he felt an almost suicidal sense of
shame for having uttered them.

"You're sorry," D'Entremont snorted. He addressed the
room at large. "Listen, this guy tries to push a man off the
goddamn dance floor and now he says he's sorry." There
was uneasy laughter. Couples stopped dancing and turned
to watch and listen. Kevin was dimly aware of being
surrounded by childlike, eager faces.

"Look," Kevin said, and was happy to discover that his
voice was stronger now, "I didn't push you. You pushed
me. Now let's forget it. We're all here to have a good
time."

Estelle had stepped to one side. D'Entremont laid his
hand, lightly, on Kevin's chest. "I hear you been tellin' lies
about me," he said. "I hear you been tellin' people I got no
guts. That right?"

"Damn it, I don't even know you," Kevin said. "I never
saw you before tonight."

"Don't take no shit off him, Kev boy," Allister called.

"You show the bastard, Kevvie," Colin shouted.

Kevin glared in the direction of their voices, hating them.
He knew now what they had been saying to D'Entremont:
"That cousin of ours, Kevin, he's been sizin' you up, Bob.
Says he's man enough to handle you." The treacherous
bastards.

"Stay out of this for God's sake," he told them. He
wondered if it were true that D'Entremont carried a knife.
"Man Stabbed to Death," he thought, two columns, two
decks, 48 Bodoni bold, with a 12-point, 22-em lead at top
left of the local page. Holy St. Kevin of Glendalough pray
for me. Holy St. Jude Thaddeus pray for me. Holy St.
Thomas Didymus pray for me. I could knee him in the
groin, but if I muffed it he'd probably knee *me* in the groin.
All ye holy saints and confessors in whom I do not believe,
forgive my unbelief and pray for me.

D'Entremont's hand became heavier, his grin broader.
"You son of a bitch," he said.

No one was dancing now. The band had stopped play-

140

ing. "Always the start was the village," and the village was waiting.

There were formalities to be observed, of course. Here such matters were governed by an etiquette that was never put into words, let alone written down. At this point I'm expected to invite him outside, Kevin thought. And when we get out there the others will make a purely symbolic attempt to prevent us from fighting. Before they stand back to watch. And the women and children will watch from the open door and from the windows, scraping away the frost with their fingernails. There will be no cheers and no hisses. And if I should happen to get him down I'll be licensed to put the boots to him, because after all he doesn't belong here, but if he gets me down, chances are Allister and Colin will interfere if he starts to put the boots to me.

And he won't dare use the knife because if he does Allister and Colin will go after him with their fists and feet and maybe even their teeth.

"You long-nosed, narrow-gutted bastard," D'Entremont said, his grin fixed, the pressure of his hand increasing.

"Leave him alone, Bob," Estelle said, "he wasn't bothering you."

He's drunk, Kevin thought. Drunker than I am. And he is almost sure that I won't fight.

"You comin' outside or ain't you?" D'Entremont asked.

"Call his bluff, Kev boy," Allister roared.

"Take him outdoors, Kev," Colin bellowed.

D'Entremont started to remove his hand from Kevin's chest.

As he did so, Kevin seized his wrist with his left hand, jerked him off balance and at the same time hit him as hard as he could with his right fist.

He aimed for the chin, but the blow struck D'Entremont's Adam's apple. As he went down Kevin aimed another blow at his face and missed. D'Entremont's head hit the side of the steel drum wood stove. He sat there, dazed, eyes wide open, a look of astonishment and almost comically childlike resentment on his face.

Now he'll get up and kill me, Kevin thought. He'll smash my testicles with his logger's boots, chew off my nose and gouge out my eyeballs with his thumbnails. Holy St. Kevin help me hit the son of a bitch over the head with a chair before he stands up.

"You want to take me home?" Estelle said, her fingers on his arm. When she touched him he realized for the first time that he was trembling.

"What?"

"You want to take me home?" she said again.

"Yeah, sure." He began to understand that D'Entremont was in no hurry to get up. His eyes were in focus now, but he had not moved. Perhaps the man was simply a coward. Perhaps he was afraid because this was Lockhartville and not Frenchman's Cross and the hall was, after all, filled with O'Briens and Foleys. Or perhaps there was not so much to this fist fighting as Kevin had believed. He was almost disappointed now that it was over. True, he had won. But his victory had been fortuitous and meaningless.

He had always imagined these, his people, battling like John Wayne and Victor MacLaglen in *The Quiet Man.* Well, at least he hadn't run, although God knows he had wanted to.

Near the door they met Allister and Colin. Their faces were almost feverish with feigned innocence. "I guess you showed that frog bastard, Kev boy," Allister said.

"Yes, sir, you took his measure, Kev," Colin agreed.

They were proud of him.

"You damn fools," Kevin said. "You crazy drunken bastards."

They punched at his head. Colin pretended he was trying to put him in a half-nelson.

> *Did you ever go into an Irishman's shanty,*
> *Where water was scarce and whiskey was*
> *plenty?*

Behind them the dancing had resumed. Kevin escaped from Allister and Colin and escorted Estelle to his rented car. They sat very close together in their heavy coats as he revved the motor and fumes from the exhaust rose around the windows like a naval smoke screen. God, it was cold. But he had never felt better.

"What are you laughin' at?" she asked, sounding either slightly worried or slightly annoyed, he wasn't sure which. It was the third time that night that he had been asked that question.

"Damned if I know," he answered.